WHISPERS
OF THE DEAD

Other books by Norma Seely:

Secrets of Harbor House
Whodunit?

WHISPERS
OF THE DEAD

•

Norma Seely

AVALON BOOKS
NEW YORK

Published by Thomas Bouregy & Co., Inc.
160 Madison Avenue, New York, NY 10016

PRINTED IN THE UNITED STATES OF AMERICA
ON ACID-FREE PAPER
BY HADDON CRAFTSMEN, BLOOMSBURG, PENNSYLVANIA

For Sharon Plumeau,
my dear friend since first grade.

Chapter One

Awakened from a sound sleep, Annie grappled with her alarm clock, knocking it to the floor before realizing the ringing she heard came from the telephone. She was totally disoriented and aware only of the thought that any phone call between midnight and six in the morning was invariably bad news. Fumbling, she finally corralled the telephone receiver and managed a mumbled, "Hello. . . ."

A voice barely more than a breathy whisper came down the telephone lines. "Annie—Annie Kirk, you've got to help me. Please—I think someone is going to kill me."

Annie pushed tangled covers away from her face. "What the . . . Who is this?"

"Annie—I think there's someone in the lodge with me. I don't know who it is. I'm scared. I'm so alone! Please, you've got to help me!"

Moonlight spilled through the window, dappling the floor and leaving a window-pane pattern on the blanket. A light breeze made the sheer curtains drift inward and Annie could hear the murmur of the ocean. "Who is this? This better not be a crank call."

"It's Trilby—you remember me, don't you, Annie? Look, I'm sorry I bothered you. It's just that I'm so scared. I'll—I'll call you back tomorrow, okay? To explain every-

1

thing." The caller didn't wait for any response but dropped the receiver in place.

Annie felt more than a moment of panic as she switched on the bedside lamp and punched * 69 in an effort to re-connect with the caller. The phone rang and rang, but no one picked up. Her foggy, sleep-clouded brain was trying to remember who Trilby was. Several seconds passed, but a face finally surfaced in her memory. Trilby Myers, of course. How could she have forgotten? Even though it had been more years than she cared to count since they'd seen one another. They'd known each other in college, hung out with the same crowd, but never been best friends. More like very good acquaintances. So was the call a malicious joke or had someone she hadn't seen or thought of in years just tried to reach her? And why—if Trilby was in trouble—had she called Annie instead of the police?

What did Trilby think Annie could do to help when she didn't have any idea where Trilby was? At least if she'd known that, she could have called the local police and asked them to contact the authorities where Trilby lived. As it was, she'd been awakened only to be made a part of someone else's nightmare. Annie reflected it was almost like a scene from one of the mysteries she wrote.

Annie sat up and rubbed her forehead. Her head ached slightly. She slipped out of bed, went into the bathroom, and found a bottle of aspirin. She had plenty of work to do come daylight and she didn't need a headache to slow her down.

Thoroughly awake now, she glanced out the bedroom window in the direction of the caretaker's cottage. There were no lights on; the place was dark as night. Which meant Brendan, who often worked on his manuscript until the wee hours of the morning, was asleep. But it didn't matter—there was nothing she or anyone could do at the moment about the totally unexpected phone call. She hadn't heard from Trilby in years, so why had Trilby suddenly picked up the phone in the middle of the night and called her? The words *I think someone is going to kill me!* kept echoing in her thoughts and pricking at her conscience even though she was helpless to do anything with the little information she had. Turning the light off, Annie crawled back into bed and lay staring into the moon-lightened darkness until a pale rose dawn threaded the eastern sky.

She gave up on the return of sleep, showered, and dressed in jeans and a light gray sweater. The day would probably warm up, but the fall morning was chilly with random wisps of fog drifting through the trees. After feeding Tiga, her cat, who had been on a midnight prowl, she brewed herself a cup of coffee and went over to awaken Brendan should he still be enjoying the luxury of sleep. She remained troubled by Trilby's unexpected phone call and wanted to share that disquiet with him. Maybe he would have a solution.

Brendan Marshall had been the caretaker at Harbor House longer than she'd been in residence. He'd taken the job because he was doing research for a biography of Hadrian Coyle, the writer of horror novels who had once owned the small estate. She'd first arrived to house-sit for a friend. Through one of those unexpected twists of fate, she now owned the property, once a lighthouse and now her private residence and a retreat for writers. Harbor House was a haven, but in the beginning she'd been stalked by terror and betrayal.

She knocked on the door of Brendan's cottage and waited impatiently for him to answer. She had to bounce the possibilities raised by last night's phone call off of somebody and he was her closest friend. She trusted and relied on him, perhaps more than she should. It was becoming increasingly difficult to imagine her life without him, and yet lately she'd sensed a degree of withdrawal on his part. He'd taken to calling her Boss Lady, which made her uncomfortable and left her wondering whether he was teasing her or defining a boundary between them.

She knocked again, this time not at all gently, and wondered when the easy camaraderie between them had changed. She couldn't imagine Harbor House without Brendan. Couldn't imagine her life without him, but she was beginning to fear that might be what he had in mind. For several weeks she'd been trying to come up with a way to approach the growing distance between them. There'd never been any declaration of love or intent. Just a growing closeness over the months that Brendan had suddenly veered away from. Perhaps she should keep last night's disturbing phone call to herself. Wait and see if Trilby called again before saying anything to Brendan.

"Are you looking for me?"

Annie turned with a start, sloshing lukewarm coffee over her wrist. Sweat beaded Brendan's forehead, stained his sweatshirt, and plastered his dark hair to his head. Obviously he'd been for his morning run. "I thought maybe you weren't up yet."

"Well, if I'm ever going to get my manuscript finished I've got to be up and at it long before you're out and about." He opened the cottage door and waited for her to enter.

"I didn't realize I was keeping you from your writing." Brendan had always appeared more than willing to help her.

"You've been keeping me pretty busy lately." It hurt him to take this firm tone with her. But he had let his infatuation, his desire to be all things to her, get in the way of the writing that was as much in his blood as her mysteries were in hers. His success was modest in comparison with Annie's, but that didn't make it any less important to him. Maybe more so, in fact, while he struggled to put himself on what he considered to be an equal footing with her. Right now she was his employer and he was never able to forget that fact, even if she could. In fairness to Annie, he suspected she never even saw their relationship in those terms. And he wished he didn't.

"I'm sorry, Brendan, if I've been asking too much of you."

"Hey, I work for you—not the other way around." Instantly he regretted his sharp tongue. Holding up the coffeepot he'd turned on before leaving for his run, he asked, "Want a refill?"

Brendan's coffee was always better than hers, and she extended her cup. "Please."

"So what brings you out so early in the morning?"

Annie sat down without invitation. "I had the strangest phone call in the middle of the night and it really has me worried. Even kept me from getting back to sleep."

"Crank call or otherwise?" Brendan poured cream in his coffee and waited for her answer.

"Well, I'm not sure." And she went on to tell him about it. "What if Trilby is really in trouble? What if I should have done something more?"

"What more could you have done? You haven't heard from her in ages. Don't even know where she lives. You'll just have to hope she calls back. Maybe she wised up and did what she should have done in the first place and called the police." He drank his coffee and watched Annie, noticing a strand of auburn hair that needed brushing away from her face and barely resisting the urge to do so. "I'm wondering why she called you when you've been out of touch for years. That strikes me as more than a little odd."

"You don't know how many times I asked myself that same question while I tried to court sleep. We haven't talked in years. And yet it's going to bother me until I find out why."

Brendan finished his coffee and set about making his breakfast. "Care to eat with me?"

Annie hesitated. "I'll pass today, thanks."

"Any chores you want done?"

There were several things, but she was still smarting from his comment he had to get up early if he was going to get any writing done. She'd never thought of herself as a slave driver, but apparently she was turning into one.

Harbor House had been standing for over a century and wasn't likely to fall down in one day. "No, none."

"Look, it's no trouble to fry an extra egg and you need more than coffee to fuel your muse. We've both got work to do and we'll do it better on a full stomach."

"I probably should go sit by the phone."

"Isn't your answering machine on?"

"Yes. . . ."

"Then this person, if she calls back, can tell you how to get a hold of her." He put two eggs in a pan and pushed the button down on the toaster.

"But what if she can't call me back? What if something really has happened to her?"

"Then there's nothing you can do about it or could have done about it. If she was in real trouble she should have called her local police." He watched her butter her toast and spread it liberally with apple butter. "Tell me about this Trilby. What was she like when you knew her?"

Annie chewed her toast thoughtfully. "As I recall, she was always part of a crowd. You see, her parents died when she was in grade school and she was shunted from relative to relative. I recall once we were all sitting around talking about what we wanted from life and she said all she really wanted was to belong to someone and some place. That comment came back to me last night when I couldn't get back to sleep because during her call she said she was so alone. Which makes me think nothing much has changed for her, and that makes me feel guilty I couldn't do anything to help last night."

"It's ridiculous for you to feel guilty over something you could do nothing about. It would just be wasted energy."

"I know, but in retrospect I realize I might have been able to get an operator to trace the call. At the time I just didn't think about it." She helped herself to more toast. "I was tempted to come talk to you, but your lights were out."

"I worked until two."

"Really Brendan, that can't be good for you to get so little sleep night after night."

"You know I've got a deadline. The publisher wants the Coyle biography to come out the same time as the unpublished manuscript you found."

"Brendan, you must say if I ask you to do too much."

"Annie—I work for you, remember." He softened his tone, even though he drove home—again—a point he felt she needed to recognize.

"I never think of it like that. I still consider that you work for the Hadrian Coyle estate."

"Yes, Annie, but last I knew you'd inherited that estate. Which makes you my boss."

She stood up, her eggs untouched. "I'm sorry that's become such a problem for you. Thanks for breakfast. Sorry, but I'm not very hungry." Her voice was as tight as the knot in her stomach.

"Annie. . . ."

She chose to ignore the plea in his voice.

As she walked through her own front door the phone was ringing. She hurried to pick it up. "Hello—"

"Annie—is that you?"

"Trilby? Where are you? You scared me half to death last night. What's going on?" Annie was filled with relief to hear her college friend had made it through the night.

"I'm sorry—really I am. I was just so frightened last night. I'm living alone in this huge old lodge in the High Cascades and sometimes at night I get a bit spooked. I'd been thinking about you during the day and planned on calling you so your telephone number was handy, scribbled on the pad beside my phone. And when I heard noises I couldn't explain, I called the handiest number. Silly of me, I know, but it's what I did."

"Wouldn't the local police have been the logical ones to call?"

"There's just a sheriff and I doubt he would have come out because I was hearing something go bump in the night."

"You said you thought someone was trying to kill you. That's hardly a bump in the night."

"You know how it is, Annie. You live alone and you get jumpy. There have been some threats, but that's probably all they are. Threats. Pranks. I haven't exactly bonded with the locals—few as they are. I just freaked out last night, and since I'd been thinking about you, you were the person I called. I didn't realize how late it was until after you'd picked up the phone."

Why had Trilby been thinking of her? At graduation they'd hugged, promised to keep in touch, but hadn't. So what did Trilby want from her now, after all this time? "So what's going on with you, Trilby? We've got a lot of years to catch up on."

"I hardly know where to begin. Let's say I've had quite a year. I was downsized from my job in Seattle and then I lost my husband."

"Oh, Trilby, no—I'm sorry, I didn't even know you were married. Was he anyone I knew?"

"No, I met Brad Watkins through a colleague at work. We'd only been married a few weeks. It was just a small ceremony before a local Justice of the Peace—no guests since neither one of us has—had—any family. Only each other."

"Would it bother you to tell me what happened?"

"He was hit by a car." Trilby's voice broke. "It's been hard. We were planning on reopening this old resort that had been in his family for years. I've tried to go ahead and implement those plans, but I'm having a little trouble getting things off the ground. That's actually why you were on my mind."

Annie wondered again what Trilby wanted from her.

"I know from the old college-friend grapevine that you run writing workshops. And of course I see your books everywhere. You're a bona-fide success, Annie." Here Trilby hesitated. "I was wondering if you'd consider holding a series of workshops here at my resort. Whispering

Pines is beautiful, especially this time of year with all the aspen turning, and your presence—hence endorsement—might be just the jump-start my venture needs."

"Well, I'm—"

Trilby didn't let her finish. "You don't have to decide right now and I'll certainly understand if you say no. I can imagine how busy you are."

"Actually I was going to say that I'm between books and have no workshops planned here for awhile. Maybe we *can* work something out." Trilby had piqued her curiosity and Annie felt like she might enjoy a reunion with her.

An hour later, the details settled, Annie was once again on her way across the yard to Brendan's cottage. Fall had laid a colorful palette of colors on the landscape and the vine maple was brilliantly red. She'd been reminding herself for days to cut a bouquet for the house but hadn't gotten around to it. The door to the cottage stood ajar and she tapped on it lightly. "Brendan? Can I interrupt you for just a minute?"

He came to the door. "What's up?"

"Trilby called me back. We've been on the phone for over an hour and I've agreed to spend three weeks at her lodge in the High Cascades conducting a series of writing workshops."

"You've agreed to do what?"

"To lead some writing workshops at her resort, Whispering Pines. Sounds like a great place, doesn't it?"

"This the same place where she claims someone is trying to kill her?"

"Frankly, I think she was being a little melodramatic. She admitted that the night and loneliness sometimes get to her."

"She sounds like bad news to me. Did she explain why she called you last night and not the police?"

"She was frightened, and having my number close at hand because she was going to call me today, dialed it. She admitted she hadn't realized quite how late it was."

"So was she just jumping at shadows or what?"

"I guess there have been some threats, but in the light of day she admitted they were probably nothing more than pranks. Living alone in such a remote location she was often uncomfortable at night."

"How remote is this resort, lodge, whatever?"

"I gather it's twenty miles from the nearest town and sits up in the timber with no close neighbors. There are hot springs on the property and one time it was run as a health spa, but that was years ago."

"And you plan on going alone?"

"Yes, I know you're busy. There's nothing much to be done around here and it'll give you plenty of time for writing. Especially if I'm not around."

"And you aren't worried at all that your friend was frightened enough about what was happening that she called you up in the middle of the night and told you someone was trying to kill her?"

"Of course I'm worried about her, but I think she was just alone and frightened. She's recently lost her husband, moved from Seattle, and the lodge is by itself in the woods. A real change from what she's used to. I know what that's like. You couldn't blast me out of Harbor House now, but in the beginning I was lonely and sometimes afraid. No doubt Trilby was exaggerating her fears, so no, I'm not worried."

"Well, I am—and invited or not, I'm going with you. I don't like the sound of this setup at all. I don't like threats, idle or otherwise. How much work will I get done if I'm constantly worrying about you?"

Chapter Two

A piercing scream echoed through the near silence of the night and stopped Annie as she was about to alight from the car. With one foot on the ground and one foot still on the floor of the passenger's side of the vehicle, she turned to Brendan. "*What* was that?" She'd been about to switch places with him and give him a much needed break from driving. Now she felt frozen in place, her breath held in anticipation of another terrifying scream that might or might not have been human.

Brendan hunched over the steering wheel in a futile effort to see into the darkness and possibly identify what they'd just heard. "I don't know what it was. It sounded like a frightened woman, but then again it was almost inhuman."

Annie shuddered, not at all comfortable to hear an echo of her own thoughts. "Don't even suggest that, please." She settled back in her seat, closed the door, and refastened her seat belt. She'd seen one scary movie too many to leave her leg dangling outside the car.

Brendan hastened to explain. "I meant it might have been an animal."

"What kind of animal would make a sound like that?" She had visions of Bigfoot emerging from the forest.

11

"I have no idea, but I don't intend to go looking in an effort to find out. Not at night and not in unfamiliar territory."

"You don't think it could have been someone in trouble?" Annie wasn't any more comfortable with the idea they might be about to ignore someone in distress than she was with the idea of plowing through the woods in an attempt to identify the source of the chilling scream.

"If it was we certainly can't do anything to help them by getting ourselves lost, but I'd be willing to bet it came from some animal." They'd been driving for hours, taking turns at the wheel, but still he was exhausted and suspected Annie must be feeling the same way. According to calculations he'd made earlier, they should have reached their destination long ago.

"I'm not so sure we aren't already lost." Annie leaned forward against her seat belt and peered into the darkness as Brendan had done earlier. It didn't help her any more than it had him. She couldn't see beyond the range of the headlights or the dark silhouettes of the trees edging the highway.

"I wouldn't go so far as to say that, but I'm betting we missed the turnoff we were supposed to take. Either that or our directions were faulty to begin with."

Just last night he'd sat at the kitchen table nursing a cup of coffee and listening while Annie talked to her friend, took down directions, crossed them out, then scribbled new instructions. She'd given him more than one exasperated look before repeating what she'd finally written down. He didn't have a good feeling about this trip east of the mountains or the late-night phone call that had started the whole process. He could ill afford the time away, yet he couldn't let Annie go on her own. What if Trilby really was in danger and that danger extended itself to Annie? He would do everything in his power to keep Annie out of harm's way.

"You heard my end of the conversation when I repeated

Trilby's directions back to her just to make sure I had them right. I didn't want us wandering around lost in the dark, because I knew we'd be arriving late. And yet here we are, in the very situation I was trying to avoid. It seems I might as well have saved my breath, because I'm inclined to agree she must have somehow misdirected us."

"You did seem to do a lot of crossing out and rewriting."

"You should have heard her end of the conversation. From the way Trilby gives directions it's a wonder to me she can even find her way home from the grocery store."

"That bad?" Brendan couldn't help chuckling.

"Yes, that bad, but when I repeated the final set of instructions back to her she didn't correct me—so I thought I had them right."

"I'm sure we'll eventually get there." A false assurance if he'd ever given one.

As they'd driven endlessly, Brendan thought of the biography he was writing about horror novelist Hadrian Coyle. He'd brought his laptop computer with him, but how much time or inspiration would he find at their destination? Hadrian Coyle was the connection that had brought him and Annie together. Which was more reason than ever to do justice to Coyle's biography.

"Brendan, we should be close to Trilby's. That scream . . . You don't think—"

"That it could have come from her? No, I don't. Not unless she's got the lungs of an opera singer. I'd lay odds it came from some animal on the prowl for its dinner. Speaking of dinner, I could certainly use some."

"Brendan, I'm sorry. I should never have let you come with me."

Just the thought of Annie in this same situation but by herself was enough to banish any regrets he might have about being there. She sounded as weary as he felt, and Brendan didn't want her to feel responsible for their present predicament. If indeed that described the situation they found themselves in. He'd be willing to bet that her scatterbrained friend was responsible if anyone was. However, he was willing to be charitable if it would put Annie's mind at rest. "There's always the possibility Trilby omitted something she didn't think was important but that would have made a difference for us. Some landmark she takes for granted and didn't think worth mentioning."

"Perhaps. . . ." But Annie didn't sound convinced. "The resort's got to be around here somewhere."

"We'll find it, don't worry." Brendan deliberately sounded more confident than he felt. Especially as prior to the scream he'd been about to suggest they look for somewhere to spend the night and continue their search for the resort in the morning. They'd passed some cabins not too far back down the road.

They hadn't seen another car for miles and the only sign of habitation had been a one-gas-pump store and cabins with a partially burned-out neon sign. Annie couldn't help but wonder what the OG IN CAFÉ was really supposed to say. Besides, she had a theory about places with partially burned-out neon signs. In her experience either the food was bad or the plumbing was backed up—or both. The night was dark as only night can be when there is the absence of light except what comes from the moon and distant stars. The heavens were beautiful, spangled as they were with starlight, but it was not a comfortable darkness as far as Annie was concerned.

After hours of driving, their destination had eluded them. Eyes had occasionally glowed at them from the roadside as they'd sped along and she'd held her breath more than once lest some animal with a death wish ran out in front of their car. Anything could hide under cover of darkness, and the scream that still had her rubbing goose bumps from her arms proved it. Something was out there and she wasn't sure she wanted to know what it was.

Again Annie leaned forward to peer out the window. "It's so dark out." She used the night to advantage in her mysteries, and it was all too easy for her to transfer danger from the printed page to reality. They were in unfamiliar country and no one, including them, knew exactly where they were. And no one but Trilby Watkins knew where they were supposed to be.

Brendan started the car up. "Look, I'm going to turn around and head back to that store and cabins we passed."

"You mean the OG IN CAFÉ?" They'd commented earlier on the partially burned-out sign.

He chuckled as she'd hoped he would. Maybe some of the unexplained tension she'd been feeling was dissipating. "That's the one. If they're still open maybe we can get some help and we can mention the scream we heard. Somebody who lives around here might know what caused it or where it can be reported. At the very least maybe we can find out if we're in the neighborhood of where we want to be. Your friend's place has got to be around here somewhere. We can't be that far off track."

"You wouldn't think so. . . ." But in the darkness and what felt like the middle of the night, who could be sure—never mind the clock on the dashboard said it was only 9:30. Annie suspected Trilby would be pacing the floor, wondering where they were. When they'd talked last, Trilby had promised to keep a pot of soup simmering on the back burner for their dinner. Neither of them had anticipated the flat tire nor the road construction that had turned a six-hour trip into an eight-hour marathon.

"If only I hadn't forgotten the cell phone! All this wondering where we are wouldn't be necessary. I could call Trilby, get directions, and put all of our minds at rest. As it is, she's probably frantic wondering when or if we're ever going to arrive." Trilby had always been a worrier, and their more recent conversations indicated she had gotten worse. Annie recalled the slightly hysterical phone call that had put her and Trilby back in touch after years of no communication. She couldn't discount Trilby's claim she was in danger, but maybe that danger was nothing more than whatever creature was behind the spine-tingling sound they'd heard a while ago. Trilby lived alone in the woods, and Annie knew better than anyone what a setting that would be for a highly active imagination.

"We did forget the cell phone, so there's no sense regretting it. We'll get where we're going eventually." Brendan wasn't one to waste much time or energy in considering what might have been. Neither was he one for looking back over his shoulder, especially not since Annie had become a part of his life. He'd led a rather itinerant lifestyle before taking the caretaker's job at Harbor House. He'd meant his time there to be spent researching Hadrian Coyle for the biography he planned to write. A stop gap before moving on to the next writing project, the next opportunity. And then he'd met Annie. He'd fallen for her on sight and couldn't do enough for her. But now it was beginning to seem she was taking him for granted. Maybe he'd deluded himself into thinking she cared for him. Maybe she really did think of him as only the caretaker. If that were the case, then he would have to think seriously about moving on. He couldn't be around her every day and *know* that she'd never be his.

The OG IN CAFÉ and cabins turned out to be about fifteen miles back the way they'd come, but luckily the OPEN sign was still lit when they pulled up. The single gas pump was a museum piece and the half dozen log cabins had definitely seen better days, particularly the one on the end with a tree through the roof. But neither of them cared because the store was still open. Annie blinked from the bright lights once they were inside. There were no shadowy corners here.

A counter and stools reminiscent of old diners stretched along one side. A luscious-looking pie with only one piece missing sat in a covered dish and half a pot of coffee simmered on a hot plate. A quick glance showed that fresh was as sophisticated as the coffee choice was likely to get. No lattes, steamers, or espressos available here. There were two booths tucked to the back, while the rest of the room was taken up by shelves heavily stocked with a variety of foodstuffs. At the moment she and Brendan were the only customers.

Annie's stomach reminded her that they hadn't eaten since mid-morning in their futile effort to make good time. "That pie looks delicious."

"And it tastes even better than it looks, young lady. Welcome to the Log Cabin Café."

Annie almost jumped at the unexpected response to her comment. She turned to find a short, rotund man with a handlebar mustache leaning against a doorway that obviously led into the kitchen.

"Ben Stokes is my name and my pies are my claim to fame. What can I do for the pair of you? Pie, coffee, sandwich? Maybe a room for the night?"

Annie was fighting the temptation to order pie and coffee when Brendan responded. "Actually, we'd just like some directions. We seem to have missed our turn-off."

The man came to lean on the counter. "Well, now, tell me where you're headed and I'll see if I can help you."

Annie reluctantly banished thoughts of immediately gratifying her hunger pangs. "We're looking for the Whispering Pines Resort. Do you know where it is? Are we anywhere near there?"

The man jerked back from the counter as if bitten and folded his arms across his chest. "Now what would you be wanting with that place?" Brendan and Annie exchanged glances. "I can offer you a snug, clean cabin and a complimentary piece of pie. Both better than anything you're likely to get at Whispering Pines."

Despite the man's belligerent attitude, Brendan managed a pleasant response. "Your offer's tempting, but we're expected at the resort. That is, if we can ever find it. Since you know of it, I take it that we're not too far away."

Ben Stokes shook his head as if their choice was beyond him. "Don't say I didn't offer you better accommodations. But it's no wonder you missed the road into it. The brush and trees haven't been cut back in years and there's no sign to mark the way. Used to be, but some vandals tore it down after all the trouble."

"Trouble? What trouble?" Annie's tone was a verbal frown. Could this man know about the threats Trilby claimed to have received? Trilby hadn't said a thing about any other trouble, unless you counted the lack of guests.

"You'd best ask that woman who's running it now. I'm not one to speculate on another's misfortune."

Annie wondered if given the time for pie and coffee she might not be able to prove otherwise. "But I take it you can tell us where the resort is."

"About a half-mile up the road, there's a turn-off on the left hand side of the highway. It's hard to find in the dark so you'll have to keep a sharp eye out." While Annie was able to rein in her curiosity, Ben Stokes wasn't. "What in the world do you want with that place anyway?" His tone wasn't that of one competitor for another, but rather one that suggested there was something wrong with Whispering Pines—something sinister, or questionable at the very least.

Annie decided there was no harm in being honest. "A friend of mine owns the resort. I understand it's been in her late husband's family for years."

He snorted. "Talk about a dubious inheritance. So you're friends with that woman who manages to drive everybody so crazy that she can't keep help, decent or otherwise. And she doesn't want to pay diddly-squat for wages. Half of the few people who book in there leave before their time is up. She's done more for my business than anything else ever did."

Brendan frowned. "What do you mean?"

"Just what I said. Never mind that nobody around here wanted to see that place reopen. People have long memories when it comes to trouble. Even if they didn't, some things are best left alone. And that would include the padlock on the front door of Whispering Pines. People went there to bathe in the hot springs and get cured of what ailed them. Well, dying is about as permanent a cure as you can get." Again he snorted. "If pines or any other tree up there could whisper maybe they'd tell what really went on at that place. And where those two women who just plain disappeared went. Never a trace found of them. So what did that old lady who ran the place do to them or with them?"

Annie felt a cold chill skitter down her spine. What did he mean that people had either died or disappeared? Trilby had never mentioned anything like that. And she relived the scream that earlier had chilled her to the bone. Maybe Trilby really was being threatened—and by someone or something not at all partial to intruders. "People have disappeared from Whispering Pines? When?"

Stokes shrugged in a non-committal manner. "It's been years ago now, but the locals don't forget. Don't reckon the next of kin to those that went missing have forgotten either. It's why the resort was closed down in the first place. That and the fact that Elmira Watkins got all strange and started talking to the dead. Or maybe it was the other way around. Maybe they started talking to her, asking her why she killed them when she was supposed to cure them."

Brendan brought his hand to rest on Annie's shoulder reassuringly. He could almost read what was going on in her very active imagination. It was what fueled the prose of her popular mystery novels, but it could also populate the shadows with menace. He did, however, spare a fleeting thought to wonder what Annie's loyalty to an old friend might have gotten them into. "But I take it this was some time ago?"

"It was, but some say you invite the dead in and it's hard to get them to leave."

Brendan decided Ben Stokes had his own issues with letting things go. "Well, I'm sure just the energy of reopening the resort has driven any unwanted guests underground."

"Where they would have stayed if Elmira Watkins hadn't gone where she had no business going. No siree! Whispering Pines is bad news and they should have burned it to the ground years ago. A good fire would have purged the place." While Stokes talked, he walked over and turned the OPEN sign to read CLOSED. "But it still stands and that's where you're headed, so I reckon you're wanting to be on your way." The words were unspoken but his tone suggested he wanted that as well.

Brendan placed his hand on the small of Annie's back and urged her toward the door. "Thanks for your help. Sorry if we kept you past closing."

As if he suddenly regretted any suggestion of bad manners, Ben Stokes said, "The pie was fresh today and will still be good tomorrow. Order a piece and the coffee's on the house."

Brendan paused before pushing open the door. "One more thing. We were pulled over to the side of the road not far from here when we heard a scream. We didn't know where we were exactly so we didn't go looking for its source. But we did wonder if it might be somebody in trouble. It wasn't like anything either of us had heard before."

"Suspect you heard a mountain lion. They can sound a lot like a frightened woman. Enough so it'll raise the hair on the back of your neck. They can also make bird-like whistles. It's just as well you didn't rush to the rescue. My recommendation is that you stay out of the woods at night and any other time if you're not an experienced hiker. But advice is cheap and I've learned people in the end do what they want to—not what you think they should. So, good luck during your stay at Whispering Pines."

The night air was brisk after the warmth of the store. Annie didn't say anything until they were once more in the car. "Now what do you make of all that?"

"That time rests heavy on Mr. Ben Stokes. Why else would he have the leisure to make up tall tales?"

"But what if there's truth to what he says?"

"There's only one way to find out and that's to ask Trilby. But even if it is true, it has nothing to do with us."

"I certainly hope not." Then, "Do you think that really was a mountain lion we heard?"

"It's a plausible explanation as far as I'm concerned." And a lot easier to live with than the thought they might have ignored somebody in trouble.

"I certainly hope we're not ignoring something we shouldn't."

"We're not. A cougar makes sense when you think about it, Annie. Remember, I said at the time I thought it sounded almost inhuman." He reached over and squeezed her hand. "Things will look better once we arrive at our destination. Which can't be far now, because that looks like our turn-off." He made a sharp left and they began bumping their way up an unpaved driveway, tree branches slapping against the side of the car.

After hitting one particularly deep pothole Annie asked, "Are you sure this is the right road? I can't imagine Trilby would have left the approach to her resort in this condition. After all, it's what's going to make the first impression."

Brendan certainly couldn't argue with her. "I was watching the mileage indicator and we'd gone half a mile when I turned off."

"Well, okay. . . ." She was dubious but would save further argument for later—if it was needed. She was really too tired at this point to be anything other than agreeable. But not too tired to be startled by a sudden flash of light just above the tree line. "What on earth was that?"

"What was what?"

"Something flashed over there above the trees. See, there it is again! Don't tell me you missed it?"

" 'Fraid so. I didn't see a thing."

"Well, I certainly did."

"Could it have been a shooting star?"

"No, it was a definite flash of light."

"Probably came from the resort. Maybe there's an outside light with a short in it."

Annie dismissed Brendan's suggestion because the light seemed to be coming from the sky. When the road made a sharp right a few moments later, her misgivings were confirmed. The only lights at the resort to welcome them came through lighted windows and from a single porch lamp. There was something else out there, something she couldn't readily explain.

Chapter Three

Brendan switched off the car engine. "Looks like we've arrived."

Annie took in the empty parking lot. "Looks like we might be the only arrivals so far. Unless there's more parking around back."

"Your friend did say she was having trouble attracting guests."

"Just as she claimed she was being threatened by someone. I had thought, hoped, she was simply being melodramatic. Maybe I've underestimated the reality of her situation." Annie thought of the succession of three workshops she had planned and wondered if anyone would show up for them. Trilby was in charge of the reservations and would describe the accommodations and how to get to the resort. No easy accomplishment in the dark. Considering the trouble they'd had following Trilby's directions, perhaps fluorescent-colored balloons tied to a tree by the turn-off might not be a bad idea.

"How can anyone expect to operate a resort when you can't find the place without a map? There should definitely be a sign down by the highway and a decent road into the property. I figured Ben Stokes was exaggerating."

Annie levered open the car door. "Me too, along with

23

those tall tales of his about people coming to the resort and either dying or disappearing. Did he truly expect us to believe all that?" Unfortunately, Ben Stokes's stories, whether true or not, had wormed their way into her already wavering expectations.

"Whether he did or not, Trilby can probably set the record straight. I imagine the main source of his discontent is the competition offered by the reopening of the resort. He certainly has bitter feelings about the place. Makes me wonder if he could be behind the threats Trilby claims to have received."

Annie was tempted to say, "What competition?" But decided to reserve judgment. She knew first impressions could be misleading and things always looked better in the daylight. "You might be right. We should be better able to tell once we pin Trilby down as to how serious the threats are. I had thought she was exaggerating out of loneliness, but now that I've seen the place and know how isolated it is, I don't know. I would never have agreed to hold the workshops if I'd thought there was any serious danger lurking around here. I've assumed all along that Trilby would have called the police if she was really, truly afraid."

Just then the front door of the lodge swung open and a slim figure came to stand against the light from the entry. Annie assumed it was Trilby, although if so, it was a much thinner Trilby than she remembered. Her college friend had always had a healthy appetite which had resulted in ample curves.

"Annie, is that you?" Whatever her current shape, there was no mistaking Trilby's little-girl voice.

"It's me—us. Did you think we would never get here?" Annie and Brendan were busy pulling suitcases and boxes from the car.

"I have to admit I was beginning to wonder. Would you like some help with your things?"

"Is there someone who could help carry them in?" Annie

had assumed from their conversations that Trilby lived here by herself.

"Only me. . . ."

"Then never mind. We'll manage." She reached for a suitcase but Brendan stopped her.

"Go up and greet your friend. I can get unloaded." Truthfully he wanted some time to himself.

"You're sure? It doesn't seem fair to make you responsible for all my stuff."

"And who better to take charge of it—and you?" His question was seriously meant, although he kept his tone light. Taking care of her was what he seemed to do best, but he didn't want to be her caretaker. No, he wanted to be her everything. He wanted to be the last person she saw before she went to sleep at night and the person beside her when she awoke. If he couldn't be that, he'd resolved to leave, as soon as this was cleared up.

Annie patted his arm. "Who indeed?" She was never certain lately how seriously she should take Brendan's comments. They seemed to have come to some sort of uncomfortable impasse in their relationship. Either he was growing tired of her company or frustrated—as she was—with the way things were. Was he really as put off by their employer-employee relationship as he'd been voicing? It just seemed so silly—unless she had been abusing her privileges. She was going to have to give it some serious thought—later when she had time to really think everything over.

Annie ran up the steps to the lodge and was immediately enveloped in an almost desperate hug. Trilby might be a fragment of her former self, but she clung to Annie as if she were drowning and Annie was a life preserver. Because of her background, Trilby had always been somewhat needy in her relationships, but never with the depth of desperation Annie was sensing now. Annie was able to break away only when Brendan reached the porch with the first of his load.

"Trilby, this is Brendan Marshall."

Trilby reached across the width of two suitcases to shake Brendan's hand, leaving him with the impression that he'd briefly held a tiny bundle of brittle sticks. He also couldn't help noticing that her clothes hung on her and her abundant blond hair was dry and lifeless. Either she was unwell or something really was amiss at Whispering Pines. What had they walked into?

"Annie tells me you're a writer also." Trilby took in Brendan's tall, muscular frame and thick dark hair appraisingly.

"Non-fiction. I'm finishing up a biography of Hadrian Coyle—or trying to anyway. I've a long way to go before I catch up with Annie."

"Well, she's certainly the most successful of our college crowd."

Annie had been glancing around the wonderful log cabin interior of Whispering Pines Resort. "Trilby, how can you say that when you're running a great place like this?"

"Running it into the ground, you mean. I can't keep help, competent or otherwise. When I do have guests they rarely stay their reservations and I have no idea why. The accommodations are rustic but comfortable, the scenery out of this world. And you know I'm a good cook. Yet people flee like rats from a sinking ship. Annie, you're looking at a desperate woman! But what kind of a hostess am I when I keep you standing on the porch after you've driven for hours and must be starved and tired? Brendan, just pile everything here in the hall and we'll take care of it after you've both had something to eat."

Annie turned to Brendan. "Are you sure you don't want me to help you?"

"Positive. I've only got another load. You go ahead."

Trilby had started to walk away but turned to say to him, "The kitchen is straight back from here. Since there's just the three of us I thought we could eat there. You shouldn't have any problem locating us." Then she laughed, sounding more like the Trilby Annie remembered. "Just follow the sounds of female chatter and you'll find us. Annie and I have a lot of catching up to do."

"Like why you never let me know you were married?"

Brendan made the one load into two, reluctant to quit the brisk, clean mountain air for the tension that wafted from Trilby like perfume. He no longer doubted that something was amiss. Maybe it was simply the lack of guests, or maybe Trilby really did feel threatened and had reeled Annie into a three-week stay as a buffer against the unknown. Which meant he not only had his manuscript to worry about, but Annie's safety as well. If there was a mystery brewing at Whispering Pines then Annie would soon be in the thick of it. And if someone was seriously intent on harming Trilby they wouldn't let an auburn-haired author of mysteries stand in their way. He well remembered the last time she'd agreed to share her expertise as a writer and instead gotten involved in a murder game that was played for real.

He lingered on the porch, drawing woodsy fresh air into his lungs and wondered if people would start showing up tomorrow or the next day for Annie's writing workshops, or if the two of them had come all this way for nothing. The first workshop was running mid-week, while the others were on the weekends. The latter were the ones he would have expected to fill up first. He scanned the heavens and wondered what had caused the flash of light Annie thought she'd seen. He had to admit anything seemed possible in a remote spot like this. Anything. He took one more deep breath and turned to go inside.

Trilby ladled steaming soup into heavy pottery bowls, then took a crisp salad from the refrigerator and a loaf of homemade French bread from a warming oven. "It isn't fancy, but I think it'll be good."

"It smells wonderful. . . ." And it did. Trilby had been a

great cook in college and it didn't look like she'd lost her touch. They'd all told her she should go to culinary school instead of opting for a business degree.

Trilby looked down at her food without interest. "I used to eat when I was nervous or upset. Now I just cook and half the time the crows get it because there's no one else around. I've purposely let myself get low on supplies so I don't waste as much. In fact, I'm going to have to go into town for groceries tomorrow." She shook her head as if her next words puzzled her. "I don't seem to have much appetite any more." Then she laughed ruefully. "That's certainly a change—isn't it?"

"Trilby, first you call me in the middle of the night claiming someone is trying to kill you. Then you tell me it's probably just a prank. I want to know the truth of what's going on. And don't try to tell me nothing because you're skin and bones."

Trilby began toying with her soup spoon. A delaying tactic both of them recognized for what it was. "When my—my husband died, I had to make some quick decisions. And one of them was whether I should move here and try to run this place on my own when we had planned to do it as a team. I optimistically assumed it would be easy to get it up and running, but it's not only siphoned off most of my money, but my energy as well. And then the threats started. Anonymous letters claiming the resort wasn't mine and that trespassers would be shot. And then there were the phone calls—heavy breathing and someone saying, 'Get out while you can! You'll never make it.' That's why I didn't pick up the phone when you said you had called me right back the other night. I was afraid it was another one of those calls."

"Surely you've reported these threats to the police."

Trilby wouldn't meet her gaze. "This is a rural, close-knit area and—and I don't want any of the locals knowing I'm having trouble. Or the guilty party finding out they're getting to me."

"Trilby, I don't think that's very wise."

"Maybe not. At this point I don't know which way to turn. I've tried to make a success of this place and so far failed. I'm about broke financially. And I can't understand what I'm doing wrong or not doing right."

"You certainly have setting and ambiance on your side. And I've only seen a fraction of what Whispering Pines has to offer."

"At first glance that's what you think, I know. But I've lived here for several months now and I'm no closer to making it pay than I was the day I moved in. And my savings are running out."

"What happened to your job in Seattle?"

"I was downsized. The city wasn't quite so exciting when I was unemployed. I was having difficulty finding another job and so I signed up for some life coaching. That made me take a long hard look at my future, particularly since I'd been married and widowed almost in the same breath. Ultimately I decided I didn't want to be in the city anymore—not with all its memories. And there was this place, which had been in Brad's family for years. I think I mentioned we had even talked about reopening it and leaving the big city. The life coaching I received encouraged me to try and run it on my own. I remember thinking, how hard could it be? I was soon to find out. Surprisingly everything was in pretty good shape. Since it had been closed up and untenanted for years that in itself was a small miracle. The old bathhouses were past salvaging, but I had no intention of trying to reopen as a health spa anyway.

"Brad's great-grandmother fancied herself as somewhat of a health guru. She was able to pull it off because those were the days when licenses and restrictions were minimal. There are hot mineral pools on the property. People used to flock here to soak in the water, which I believe *is* beneficial to joint ailments. But even thinking about reopening that end of the business is overwhelming. The bathhouses would have to be rebuilt. Then I'd have to hire competent personnel and jump through all the hoops necessary to get approved. I have enough trouble getting and keeping employees as it is."

"Why is that, do you have any idea?" Annie recalled Ben Stokes's assertion that her friend didn't pay a competitive wage.

Trilby stirred her cooling soup but didn't meet Annie's gaze. "I guess nobody wants to work here anymore. The resort is rather remote. I did have a manager lined up. He was living on site and was going to handle the actual day-to-day running of things. I couldn't afford to pay him very much beyond room and board, but he wanted a job that would allow him the time to pursue his art while still providing him with a roof over his head." Then she added unnecessarily, "He was an artist, but he seemed organized enough to help me run the place. And he had resort work experience."

Annie couldn't help but notice Trilby's use of the past tense. "What happened to him?" Brendan had just appeared in the hallway behind Trilby but she said nothing for fear of distracting her friend.

Trilby glanced up from her soup stirring and the expression on her face was one of misery. "I don't know what happened to him."

"You don't know?"

"He simply disappeared."

"You mean he walked off the job?"

"I don't know if that's what happened to him or if . . ." She didn't finish her thought.

Brendan served himself some soup and then sat down at the worn, round table. "Are you suspicious that something might have happened to him?"

"I don't know. I *just* don't know. It seems unlikely anything could have without my knowing it. But there are so many things around here that don't seem to have a logical explanation. When I leave for any length of time I'd swear someone is getting inside and stealing food. Not a lot, but enough that I know I haven't miscalculated on amounts. And when I come back there's that feeling you get when you just know someone has been there. Little things are out of place, like a glass left beside the sink when I've washed everything up." She took a deep breath. "And then there are the items that have gone missing."

Brendan's tone was sharp as he asked, "What kinds of things?"

"Small things—earrings, slips of paper. Actually, things that could be easily misplaced. I suppose that's the only thing that has saved me from a lawsuit. One of my few guests claimed someone stole one of her diamond stud earrings. We searched high and low but couldn't find it. But since only one of them was missing it seemed unlikely that anyone had taken them. I mean, why take one earring?"

"So you think she probably just lost it?"

"I don't know, Annie. I really don't. I anticipated problems when I decided to reopen the resort, but never the kind I've faced. There was a lot of deep cleaning that needed to be done before I could open, so I went to the employment agency in the nearest town. They sent me several applicants, only one of whom stuck around long enough to do any real work. And I was paying the going rate for housekeepers so that couldn't have been the problem."

"Couldn't you have gotten replacements?"

"I tried, but when I contacted the employment agency they said they couldn't persuade anyone to come up here. When I pressed them as to why, I was finally told it was because the women felt uncomfortable here."

Annie glanced at Brendan. "Uncomfortable? What did they mean by that?"

"Believe me, I tried to find out. I felt I had a right to know what was keeping workers away or what was being said. How was I ever going to get this place up and running if I couldn't get any help? When I got nowhere with the employment agency I contacted the women themselves.

Some of them wouldn't talk to me, but the one who did simply said there was something strange about this place. That she'd heard stories in the past about the 'goings-on' up here, but that she hadn't believed them until she came to work here."

Annie frowned in puzzlement. "Did she give you a clue as to what she meant?"

Trilby laughed half-heartedly. "Only that she kept seeing this face at the window. And of course the threats I'd been receiving weren't all confined to paper. Sometimes they were scrawled on the windows or on the driveway in chalk. Frankly, I think they were afraid of the fallout should something happen to me."

"What do you think is behind these happenings?" Brendan asked.

"I think someone doesn't want me to reopen the resort. That they're deliberately trying to sabotage me. They know I live alone here and they think they can frighten me away."

Ben Stokes's image flashed through Annie's thoughts. "What reason would anyone have for wanting to do that? Has someone tried to buy you out and when they couldn't resorted to other tactics?"

"No, no one. At times I've almost wished someone would and then I'd have enough money to start over again somewhere else. This remote existence is a far cry from the life I lived in Seattle."

"Why should someone repeatedly accuse you of trespassing?"

"I don't know, Brendan. I have as much right to be here as anyone."

"Then tell me, Trilby, do you want this venture to succeed or not?"

Trilby pushed her chair away from the table and got up to empty her barely touched bowl of soup into the sink, then refilled Brendan's bowl without asking him if he wanted more. "I've asked myself that question more than once, believe me. When I was downsized from my job I had a substantial savings account and a generous severance package. As I mentioned, coming here was a way of holding on to Brad through implementing the dream we had planned." She was silent for a moment. "I had thought I might do a bit of freelancing—and odd jobs if necessary. Then I realized I couldn't do that and try to reopen the lodge. Plus I have to admit I liked the idea of sharing my space with others. It's a bit big for one person—and I might as well admit it, a little isolated. My nearest neighbor is the guy who runs the Log Cabin Café and I can't say we've exactly bonded."

"We stopped there for directions when we couldn't find the turnoff."

"Then you've met him. I'll bet if you told him where you were headed he tried to discourage you."

Good, Annie thought, here's an opening. "Why do you think he would do that?"

"I could say that he's afraid of the competition—but since I haven't provided any I don't know what the reason might be."

Brendan didn't believe Trilby could be ignorant of the resort's past when it had been in her late husband's family for generations. "Stokes mentioned that there'd been some trouble associated with the resort."

"Oh, he went out of his way to tell you that, did he?"

"I wouldn't say he went out of his way. We asked for directions and he gave them to us. Mentioning in the process that vandals had torn down the sign by the highway after all the trouble."

"And did Stokes elaborate?"

Annie could tell that Trilby was getting upset at Brendan's questions. She didn't want them getting off on the wrong foot—not when they were scheduled to stay for three weeks. Especially when Brendan seemed to have left his usual easygoing attitude at home. "No, he didn't. He said if we wanted to know then we should ask you."

Trilby sighed and pushed her hair away from her face.

"Well, you can ask me, but I don't know that I can tell you much. The lodge had been empty for over twenty years. Ever since Brad's great-grandmother passed away. Brad's folks would come up for a few weeks each fall, but for the most part it was shuttered and bolted. And he and I came up a couple of times. So I wasn't unfamiliar with the layout of the place when I moved in."

"So when did the place last operate as a spa?" Annie asked.

"In Brad's great-grandmother's day. She passed away in '79. The lodge had been left to her sons, but both of them were dead, so Brad's father inherited it. At least I think that's how it went."

"And no one ever attempted to sell it?"

Trilby shook her head at Brendan's question. "Brad's father never wanted to. I think he had hopes of retiring here."

"What happened that he didn't?"

"He and Brad's mother were killed in a plane crash on the way to Brad's college graduation. I think Brad kept the lodge because it was a way of keeping their memories alive. Just as I've kept it because it was part of his family history and I really have none of my own. But," and she leaned with her back against the sink while drying her hands, "if I can't make it pay then I'll have no option but to try and sell it."

Annie wondered how many guests Trilby had actually hosted. "Have you had many reservations yet?"

"You mean for the workshops?"

Had Trilby deliberately misunderstood her? "I meant period."

"I've had a grand total of half a dozen guests and I've been open for business five months. Two of them were a young couple who got their information from old brochures and didn't bother to ask me if the bathhouses were still in use. They soaked in the hot springs for a couple of days and then moved on. Seems they make a habit of visiting different hot springs and they were a bit miffed that all I had available were the springs themselves. No hot mud soaks or massage therapists. The other four were bored silly within five minutes. It seems they expected me to provide entertainment for them. Monopoly on a card table before the fire wasn't quite what they had in mind." Trilby smiled at the memory. "But you know, I viewed both instances as a learning experience. Many people do expect more than just a place to lay their head. That was when I hit upon asking you to conduct some writing workshops. If I can just get a name going for myself, then I think I can make the resort work. That night I called you, I'd been mapping out what I would say to persuade you to come here. I'd even written myself a little script. That's why your number was so handy for me. Why I called you when I thought I heard someone. . . ."

Trilby was just reiterating what she'd already explained. Annie wasn't about to question her logic on guests, although she thought there were a good many people who would be glad to simply enjoy the relaxed beauty of Whispering Pines. But Trilby needed to make the most of the resort's natural attributes. "And have we had any takers for the workshops?"

"You said you didn't want any more than half a dozen for each session and we almost have that for the first one."

Almost enough? Annie never had trouble filling her workshops at the beach, although this was the first time she'd tried holding one mid-week. "Are we ready for them?"

"The rooms are spic and span with fresh linens and bars of pine-scented soap in the bathrooms."

"Remember, we promised them light meals."

"I have that covered, or I will have after a trip to the supermarket tomorrow."

Annie thought that was cutting it a bit close. "We need to have everything in place before the participants start to arrive."

"I have menus planned and I'll do the shopping tomorrow. Then I'll get started on the baking."

"You're sure doing all the cooking won't be too much work for you?" Annie didn't like the exhausted look of her friend. Would Brendan, whose past included experience as a short-order cook, step into the fray and help? She glanced in his direction but said nothing.

Brendan knew from Annie's expression that she was wanting him to save the day by offering to help in the kitchen. A responsibility he couldn't take on if he was going to get his manuscript finished. She was so used to him picking up the pieces that she didn't stop to think there might be things he considered more important. He had only himself to blame, because in his affection for Annie he'd bent over backward to help her out and to be with her. However, he shared her obvious worry about Trilby's ability to fulfill her part of their agreement. "I can help by going to the store if you'll give me a list. That way you can get started with the baking. And why don't I pick up some deli trays? That should take the work out of lunches."

An enormous look of relief spread over Trilby's face, but she glanced at Annie for approval. "Would that be all right with you, Annie? It certainly would make things easier for me."

"Whatever works is fine." Annie knew Brendan wouldn't stint while he was at the store, but she was a little surprised he hadn't offered to actually help with the cooking. He certainly fed her often enough when they were at Harbor House, since her own idea of preparing a meal was to open a can. But then maybe he didn't feel Trilby's responsibilities should become his. And he was right, although Annie suddenly felt as if she'd lost something. To cover her feelings of confusion, or maybe to hide them from herself, she changed the subject. "Trilby, as we drove up, I noticed a flash of light in the night sky. Do you know what might have caused it?"

"No—no I don't. I noticed them when I first moved here,

but anyone I asked for an explanation said folks around here had learned to ignore them."

"That seems strange. I'd think people would want to get to the bottom of them."

"I really don't think they're anything to worry about."

"I'm not worried, but I certainly am curious."

Brendan stretched and yawned. "It's been a long drive and I'd like to get some sleep. Just point me in the direction of my room and you two can sit up and visit as long as you want."

"I think it will be easier if I show you where you're staying." And as if she feared a late-night chat with Annie would bring more probing questions, Trilby added, "You might as well come along, Annie, so I can show you to your room also. I'm sure you're tired out as well."

Yes, Annie was tired, but she had been in hopes she and Trilby could catch up a bit on each other's lives. She'd always felt a little sorry for Trilby, and that hadn't changed. But apparently Trilby didn't feel like catching up. It was late, but not that late. "Just let me get a drink of water and then I'll be along. I'll be with you shortly, don't worry."

"The glasses are in the cupboard by the sink."

Annie found them without any trouble and was drinking deliciously cool water when she saw another light ripple across the sky. She realized it was probably only her imagination or the fact that she was really, really tired, but it seemed the floor beneath her feet shifted slightly.

Chapter Four

Annie slept soundly, only waking when the roar of a vacuum cleaner disturbed her sleep. She sat up, puzzled by the unfamiliar surroundings before realizing where she was. Sunlight filtered through wavy window panes and the fresh scent of piney woods drifted in through the open window. Laying back against the pillows, she stretched and took inventory of the room that would be her home for the next three weeks. Last night she'd been so exhausted she'd done little more than take a quick look around, but now she could see the room matched the downstairs in rustic authenticity.

The double bed was comfortable with just the right amount of downy comforters to ward off the chill fall air. The bed itself was fashioned from peeled logs turned a buttery yellow with age. Pictures of canoes gliding across pristine lakes and elk grazing in grassy meadows hung on the opposite wall. Their frames were constructed from bark and tree limbs and decorated with a border of what looked like pine needles. Faded plaid curtains hung at the windows, and a lamp shaped like a bear catching a fish sat on the pine nightstand that matched the bureau. Annie fell totally in love with her surroundings and wondered if Trilby was too wrapped up in her problems to appreciate the treasure she'd inherited. But then who wouldn't be, given the threats she claimed to have received and the loss of her husband when their marriage was only a few weeks old.

If properly run, Whispering Pines should be a gold mine. Annie couldn't understand why each and every room wasn't filled. There had to be more to the situation than Trilby had told them and Ben Stokes had hinted.

Annie had her own postage-stamp-size bathroom, and she took full advantage of a hot shower even though there was scarcely room enough to turn around in the shower stall. The light over the sink cast flattering shadows along her high cheekbones and made her auburn hair look even darker. She brushed it thoroughly, twisted it up into a knot on her head, then applied the light amount of makeup to her face that always made her feel equal to greeting the day.

The only fault she could find with her accommodations was the lack of heat, and she supposed that was one place where Trilby was economizing. It was also something she'd have to correct if she wanted to encourage guests. Annie was thankful she'd packed several warm sweaters. Shivering in her underwear and jeans, she rooted through one of her suitcases until she found a heavy fisherman's knit sweater and thick socks. On a glorious morning like this and in this beautiful mountain country, she had to start her day with a walk. Once the workshops started there probably wouldn't be time for such a luxury. Even though she allowed the workshop participants plenty of down time to relax and absorb what they were learning, someone always sought her out with questions during this time. Which left her little or no time for relaxing.

The vacuum was still whirring away when she stepped into the hallway and she was surprised to find that it wasn't Trilby, but another woman who switched off the vacuum when she saw Annie. "You must be that writer lady I've been hearin' so much about."

"Guilty." Annie extended her hand. "I'm Annie Kirk."

The woman wiped her hand on her jeans before taking hold of Annie's. "I'm Maxine Polk, the only housekeeper with guts enough to keep comin' back here. Or should I say the only housekeeper who's hungry enough to keep showin' up for work."

Annie sensed here was a source of information. She could smell a mystery, and the best way to solve a mystery was to ask questions. Ben Stokes had mentioned trouble at the resort; Trilby said that she had received threats and her manager had disappeared; and now Maxine Polk claimed she was the only housekeeper with guts enough to stick around. So what was the real truth behind all of this? Annie wanted to know—was determined to find out. After all, for the next three weeks she had a vested interest.

"Trilby did mention she was having trouble getting help."

Maxine leaned against her vacuum. "It isn't so much that she's havin' trouble gettin' help, but that she's havin' trouble keepin' it."

Annie succumbed to temptation without even a second thought. "Do you know why that is?"

Maxine dug in her pockets and unwrapped a piece of gum. "People around here have long memories and they remember all the trouble that went on before. As a kid I heard stories about this place. Every community has its haunted house and this place filled the bill. Nobody had lived here for years, but old-timers still talked about Elmira Watkins bein' crazy as a loon. I guess she made some pretty fantastic claims for those hot springs out back and for her own health regimen. Near the end she's supposed to have starved people to death all the while claimin' she was makin' them well."

"Maxine, surely you don't believe those stories?" Annie knew the most bizarre things were often accepted as truth without a shred of proof.

Maxine shrugged. "I'm just tellin' you what I've heard. I do know an awful lot of people are just plain desperate when it comes to their health. And they'll do anything if they think it might help them feel better. This was supposed to be a health spa, and I suppose they thought old Elmira knew what she was talking about. Whether you believe that or not is up to you. But if it's proof you want of what went on here, there's documented evidence in the newspapers that two women did disappear while they were stayin' here. Went out for a walk and flat out never came back. That kinda put people off when the word got out."

"But that wasn't the fault of the resort. Unless the women had been locked in their rooms Elmira couldn't have kept them from walking in the woods."

Maxine shrugged again. "Fault or not, she's the one who got the blame. And how do we know they went walkin' in the woods? One of her so-called cures might have done them in and she just told people they went for a walk and didn't return. Maybe they're buried somewhere out back. Or lyin' in the bottom of one of those hot springs with a rock around their neck to keep them from floatin' to the surface."

Good grief, thought Annie, if anyone should be signed up for a mystery writing workshop it was this housekeeper. "Is that what you think, Maxine?"

"It don't matter what I think. As long as my paychecks don't bounce I'm a happy camper. But—I could tell you things." And she popped her gum.

Annie was about to say, "Then why don't you?" when Maxine quickly switched on the vacuum and went about her business.

It wasn't hard to guess that Trilby was approaching. Annie turned to greet her college friend. "Good morning."

"Annie, did you sleep well? I see you've met my housekeeper."

"I slept like the proverbial log and yes, I've met Maxine. We were getting acquainted."

"I can just imagine." Trilby took hold of Annie's arm. "Let's go downstairs and have a cup of coffee." When they were out of Maxine's hearing she added, "Maxine loves to gossip so don't pay much attention to anything she says. Give her a tidbit of information and she'll turn it into an epic novel."

"She seems efficient enough."

"Oh, I can't fault her cleaning skills. I have the cleanest hall carpet in the county. I just don't want to pay her to stand around and talk. Since she's the only housekeeper who keeps coming back she has plenty of work to do."

Annie almost felt as if she herself had been rebuked for taking up a few minutes of Maxine's precious time. "As do we. Shall we touch base on the workshops?"

"Definitely. I'll make us some fresh coffee and then we can go over the reservations that have come in so far."

They reached the spacious, old-fashioned kitchen and Trilby set about making coffee. "I can offer you a fresh-baked cranberry scone or cereal. I'm out of everything else."

"A scone will be fine. You might remember that I don't eat much breakfast." But since Brendan was a two-eggs-over-easy, whole-wheat-toast, and fresh-fruit guy, she wondered how he would fare.

The coffee was soon done, and after pouring them each a cup Trilby said, "I'll go get the reservations that have come in so far and be right back."

She was as good as her word, but Annie saw with disappointment that there were only a few. Well, Trilby had warned her last night. "Is that it?" She couldn't keep the dismay from her voice.

Trilby laid them on the table and nodded. "That's it. But you did say you didn't want any more than six people in each workshop, and this is five."

"Yes, but I would like six. That's kind of the break-even point. And we're offering three workshops. I had expected them to be filled by now." She was more than a little disappointed, but when she saw her own reaction mirrored on

Trilby's face she added, "Perhaps more will arrive in to-day's mail."

"Maxine brought the mail up when she came to work today. So this is it—so far."

"Well, it looks like we'll have to make do with five participants. By the way, where *do* you pick up your mail?"

"My mailbox is down on the highway. Usually I walk down and get it, but Maxine picks it up the days she works. You aren't going to cancel the workshops are you?" Trilby's voice took on an edge of panic. She was holding on for dear life to the thought that Annie and Brendan would be with her for the next three weeks.

Annie administered a reassuring verbal pat on the back. "No, of course I won't cancel. I can use a vacation even if the workshops don't fill up completely."

Trilby seemed to relax. "I sent confirmations out to these people as you requested. And I included maps on how to get here."

"That's a good idea. It will be even better if everyone arrives during daylight." She'd hate to think anyone else would stop at the OG IN CAFE for directions, where they'd end up with a dose of Ben Stokes's unabridged gossip. She reached for the envelope on top. "Okay, let's see who we have here. Jocelyn Curtiss from Bend. Well, she won't have far to come. Who's next?"

Trilby handed her the second reservation. "This is Jackie Marks from Seattle." Then she opened the next one. "Carmen and Frank Potts from Medford. They included a little note."

Annie took the piece of paper from Trilby. Carmen Potts wrote that she and her husband had written several successful romance novels under the name Daphne Moore. Now they were ready to try their hand at a mystery. "Well, they should be interesting."

"So should this woman."

Louella Haven stated she was seventy-five years old and had always wanted to write a mystery. " 'I figure I've got at least one good book-length story in me.' " Annie glanced up. "She sounds like fun."

"So you will go ahead with the workshops? There are enough people for this first one?"

"Trilby, don't fret. I agreed to do them and I will. I sent out brochures to all the people on my mailing list, which is made up of people who've attended previous workshops or who've asked to be notified of future offerings. Lots of people wait until the last minute to register. There are those who show up at the door unannounced even though the brochures plainly state they need to pre-register." Annie was, however, more than a little surprised at the poor response. Her workshops at the coast generally had a waiting list.

"What do you do with those people?"

"What?" Annie had been thinking ahead, wondering if there was anything she could do to jump-start enrollment for the second and third sessions.

"What do you do with people who just turn up the day of the workshop? Do you let them attend?"

"I've never turned anyone away, but I do charge them a late registration fee. I don't have much patience with people who don't read the fine print. Or who ignore it once they have, thinking it doesn't apply to them." Especially as these were often the people who monopolized every conversation and asked innumerable questions—pertinent or not—just so the spotlight would be on them.

"I just wondered how to deal with the situation should it arise. In case you're not around."

"Tell me, Trilby, won't you and Maxine need some help once people start showing up? We've promised them room and board as well as the workshop. There's bound to be extra laundry and people will probably expect their rooms to be cleaned each day."

"The rooms are all ready and I think Maxine and I can manage between us. Surely people won't expect anything more than their beds made and fresh towels put out. It's only for two days at a time, we'll manage—don't worry."

But when Annie looked at the once pleasingly plump, now overly thin, weary-looking Trilby she couldn't help but be concerned. Trilby didn't look up to the stress Annie knew accompanied the workshops. Life, and Whispering Pines, seemed to have taken a toll on her friend. Her musing was abruptly put on hold when the telephone at the front desk rang, startling them both. It was the first time she'd heard it ring since arriving the night before.

Rather than jumping up, Trilby turned to her. "Annie, would you get that for me, please? It's probably someone about the workshops anyway."

Annie wondered if Trilby was afraid it might be another threatening call. Was there anything she could do to get to the root of them? She remembered only too well the stalking that had caused her to seek sanctuary at Harbor House and had her jumping at shadows for months. "Sure, I'll get it." She hurried to the lobby and caught the phone on its fifth ring. "Whispering Pines Resort, may I help you?"

"Well, I certainly hope so. My name is Fran Shipman and I sent my reservation in for that writing workshop weeks ago and still haven't heard a word back. I thought I'd better make certain you're expecting me before I head out. I don't want to drive all the way over there and find out the thing's been cancelled or you don't have room for me."

Having just gone over the meager list of people who had sent in reservations, Annie could reply with authority. "I'm really sorry, but we never received your reservation. If you want to give me the information over the phone I can register you now. There's still one slot available."

"Never received it? How could that be? I mailed it weeks ago. That doesn't sound very efficient to me. Well, never mind. I want to come for the first session. Am I too late for that one?"

"No, that will work out fine. You should already have

the necessary information so you know what to bring with you."

"Yes, do I pay by credit card or check when I get there?"

Annie knew Trilby wasn't set up for credit cards—a mistake as far as Annie was concerned—but a fact they had to deal with. "By check when you get here will be fine."

"Very well—and who am I talking to?"

"Annie Kirk—and I'm looking forward to meeting you."

Suddenly the woman's snippy tone mellowed. "Oh, the author. Oh, my goodness, I just *adore* your books."

"Thank you—I'm always glad to hear that." Which was certainly true enough. "We'll see you then and I look forward to meeting you." Then she remembered that the maps on how to reach the resort were included with the reservation confirmations. "You'll need directions on how to get here. They would have been included in your confirmation packet."

"The address is on the brochure. Am I apt to get lost?"

"Let me give you a bit more explicit directions if you have a pen and paper handy."

"I do."

Annie then told her in detail how to find the lodge. "You shouldn't have any trouble especially if you arrive during daylight."

"I always try to do that. So, if that's it, I'll see you soon."

"Just come prepared to enjoy yourself and to plot a crime. You'll go home with the outline for a novel."

"I will?" The woman sounded absolutely thrilled. "Oh, my goodness, I hadn't expected quite that much."

"You'll work hard, but you'll get your money's worth—I promise."

"That's wonderful, Annie. I can hardly wait to meet you." The woman was genuinely enthusiastic, which was music to Annie's ears.

"And I look forward to meeting you." Annie hung up the telephone with a sigh of satisfaction. She was glad to have the first workshop filled, but she was a bit curious as to what had happened to Fran Shipman's reservation. What if more applications had gone astray and at the last minute they had an overflow turnout? She could always adjust her material, but Trilby only had so many rooms available.

Now that she was in her workshop-thinking mode, Annie looked around the small lobby with an eye to making it a bit more inviting. She wanted a welcome sign and a display of other workshop information. And she'd learned from experience that people expected her to have copies of her books for sale. The reservation desk would be a good place for this since the guest book on a revolving pedestal didn't take up much room. Behind the counter there were cubbyholes for mail, and across from there a grouping of leather chairs and a stone fireplace. If it was operational, a fire would be a nice touch. After all, most of them would have a long drive behind them when they arrived. There would even be room on the counter for a plate of cookies, cups and carafes of coffee, and hot water for tea. It was important to get off to a good start by making people feel welcome.

She was about to confirm these arrangements with Trilby when the toe of her shoe prodded something soft. Glancing down she spotted a very dead rat. If she'd brought her cat with her instead of boarding him, she would have blamed the corpse on him. Lacking a scapegoat, she looked around for some way to dispose of it. Luckily it hadn't started to smell. But there was nothing adequate to pick it up with and she was about to head for the kitchen and some paper towels when Trilby appeared.

"What's taking so long? Who was on the phone. . . ." Then she noticed what lay at Annie's feet. "Oh, ick! Where did that come from?"

"I have no idea, but I'll get rid of it as soon as I find something to pick it up with." It was then she noticed a large pad of paper shoved back under the counter. Pulling it out, she flipped it open and was about to remove a page when she saw that it was somebody's sketch pad. "Trilby, is this yours?" The drawings were exceptional.

Trilby came over to see what she'd found. "Oh, good heavens no. That belonged to Big Al, my erstwhile manager. I didn't realize that was there. I told you he was a professional artist and took this job mainly to have a place to live."

"Big Al? He sounds like a gangster."

Trilby laughed. "No, that's just what everybody calls him. He's well over six feet tall with a husky build." She stood beside Annie as she slowly turned the pages of the sketch pad.

"Trilby, these are breathtaking." And they were. "Look at this—" The drawing that had caught her attention was that of a woman, or actually the outline of her kneeling form, apparently carved into a large rock. A clearing extended beyond her, while mountain peaks seemed to disappear into a haze. "I wonder where this is? It's so beautiful, but at the same time haunting. I wonder what she's doing?" It was hard to tell if the woman was sleeping, praying, or perhaps weeping, for her head rested on one folded arm.

"Oh, that subject again."

"What do you mean? Have you seen something like this before?"

"That rock sculpture is a part of local lore. Somebody probably told Al about it and he drew this picture from his imagination."

Annie wasn't about to argue; after all Trilby knew the artist and she didn't. But the drawing had a sense of reality about it, a degree of detail that suggested the artist had been recording something he wanted to remember. The kneeling woman fascinated Annie and she wondered if it was to be found anywhere near the lodge.

Trilby stepped away, having lost interest. "We need to get rid of this rat. Just tear a page out of the reservation log to pick it up." Her face took on a thoughtful expression.

"I still have hopes Al will come back. He left quite a few things here. . . ." her voice wandered off as if following Al into the unknown.

While Trilby considered the possible fate of Big Al, Annie scooped up the rodent. "What would you like me to do with this?"

"Just put it in the garbage can outside the back door."

Annie deposited the carcass in the trash and then returned to the kitchen and the subject of the missing manager. "You did report your concerns to the police, didn't you?"

Trilby's sheepish expression was all the answer she needed. Nevertheless, her friend sought to justify herself. "You had to know Big Al. He was—is—pretty much a free spirit. And when he's in a creative mode he doesn't even know you're around."

"Trilby, did he leave everything behind?" Annie was starting to question Trilby's lethargy regarding her AWOL manager and to wonder why she hadn't contacted the local police.

"No, no he took some things. It was mainly artwork he left behind."

Annie felt a rush of relief. "Then we're not really looking at a missing person?"

"Probably not. I guess I use the term *missing* rather loosely. That's why I didn't contact the police, because I'm sure there must be a logical explanation as to where he's gone."

"I thought from the way you'd talked that he practically vanished into thin air." Would there turn out to be as simple an explanation behind the anonymous threats Trilby feared? Still. . . . "It seems a bit strange that he didn't at least say good bye."

"That's what I thought, especially since he did have some wages owed him and didn't leave any forwarding address. But you know how creative people can be." Suddenly realizing what she'd said, Trilby hastily added. "Oh, I don't mean you, Annie. You're very responsible."

Annie wished she could say the same about Trilby. "What do you say we get on with arrangements for the workshop. I think a plate of cookies and carafes of coffee and hot water would be nice on the counter in the lobby. Most everyone is coming some distance and a bit of readily available light refreshment is always welcome. It does wonders for morale. Also I was wondering about a fire in the fireplace."

"We certainly could, but it still gets quite warm around here during the day."

"I hadn't thought about that. Perhaps we can have one if the evenings are as cool as last night."

"Whatever you want, Annie."

"I guess that about does it. Have you seen Brendan yet this morning?"

"No, I haven't."

"He's probably gone for his morning walk." She was missing his company. "By the way, that phone call was from a Fran Shipman who wondered why she'd never gotten a confirmation for the workshop reservation she'd mailed in. I explained we'd never received it, but that there was room for her. So we're full for the first session. But I can't help wondering where her reservation went. Is the name at all familiar to you?" Annie hadn't discarded the possibility that Trilby might have received and mislaid reservations.

Trilby shrugged. "No, it's not. She probably put the wrong zip code on the envelope and it will eventually show up."

"At least she called when she didn't receive a confirmation. I wouldn't want too many surprises of that nature." As soon as the words were out of Annie's mouth she regretted them when she saw Trilby's brow furrow and a worried expression settle over her friend's face.

"Oh, I hope not too. I only have nine rooms. Oh, my

goodness, I never thought of that happening. What would we do?"

"Make the best of it. But don't worry, I'm sure that's not going to happen." Regardless of what she told Trilby, Annie couldn't shake a certain feeling of concern that other reservations might have been lost or perhaps taken from the mailbox beside the highway. It was very unusual for her workshops not to fill up. Whispering Pines Resort had a glorious setting, and autumn in the High Cascades was hard to beat for color, warm days, and crisp nights for sleeping. The price was exceptional, especially as it covered not only the workshop, but food and lodging. People should be standing in line to attend.

Hearing the sound of a distant vacuum, Annie made a spur-of-the-moment decision. "Trilby, keep my coffee warm, I'll be right back."

Maxine saw Annie approach and switched off the vacuum. Either she had a sixth sense or she was hoping for another quick gossip. "Breakfast over?"

"As of yet it hasn't started. Maxine, I'm a little concerned as it seems at least one, if not more, of the reservations for my workshops have gone astray. Trilby tells me you and she share the mail pickup duties. I don't want to worry her any more than she appears to be already. Do you think it possible that someone could be removing mail from the box? It's certainly accessible and there's no close neighbors to see if someone was practicing a little theft. You've suggested, and so has Ben Stokes at the Log Cabin Café, that the locals have it in for the resort. Do you think that could result in a little mail theft? You're in a far better position than me to know what's going on around here and how far vindictiveness might go."

Maxine absently unwrapped a stick of gum. "I suppose that's always possible. Kids lookin' to make a little mischief. But you know, Miz Watkins has a habit of puttin' things down and then forgettin' where she put them. She's always askin' me if I've seen something or moved something. So you might want to just have a good look around. And I'll keep an eye out myself. I don't go through any of her personal papers, but if I see any unopened mail in unlikely places, I'll take a peek."

"Would you please." Annie realized she'd just sanctioned snooping, but it seemed like it was for a good cause. "It doesn't get the workshop off to a good start if I have to greet people with the information that I never received their reservation. It upsets them and makes me—us—look somewhat incompetent."

"I'm everywhere in this place, so I'll just keep my eyes open." And with that, Maxine switched the vacuum back on. As she moved on down the hall, Annie thought Whispering Pines must have the cleanest floors around. She had as yet to see Maxine without a vacuum cleaner.

Annie had turned and started downstairs when she turned back toward Maxine, talking loud enough to be heard above the vacuum. Maxine switched it off and waited expectantly. "Is there something else?"

"Maxine, do you know anything about a rock carving of a kneeling woman?"

"Most folks around here do, although they'd be hard pressed to take you to it. My grannie told me she represented a Paiute princess."

"But you don't know where it is?"

" 'Fraid not. More than one person's gotten in trouble lookin' for her though. Like those two women who disappeared all those years ago from this resort. They were supposed to be lookin' for her and they never came back."

Chapter Five

"You're not suggesting there was any kind of connection?"

Maxine shrugged and popped her gum. "Well, nobody I know of has ever seen it—her."

"Trilby's manager left behind a sketch pad that contains a drawing of the sculpture."

"Yeah, and do any of us know what became of him? One day he's here, the next he's gone with nary a word to anyone. People who go lookin' for that rock carving don't seem to come back."

Annie suspected Maxine was having a bit of fun with her. "Trilby says he took most of his things with him."

"She tell you that? Then what's all that stuff she had me move out of his room and into the attic?" When Annie said nothing in return, Maxine nodded her head in satisfaction, switched on the vacuum, and began working her way down the hall.

Annie stood for several seconds wondering how much of what she was hearing was truth and how much embroidered with the imagination of time. One thing was for certain, she was going to have a look in the attic before she left Whispering Pines.

For years the resort had operated as a health spa, which

would mean a procession of sick people passing through its doors. Wasn't it natural to assume that for some of them the resort was a last hope at regaining their health? Wasn't it also logical to assume some of them might not have left alive? Wouldn't the building have absorbed at least some of the suffering that passed along its halls? Was Trilby, already suffering her own loss, feeling the weight of all that had happened here? Or was there something more sinister at work?

Brendan pushed open the front door just as Annie reached the bottom of the stairs. As always, she felt an inward lift of spirits when she saw him and hoped that perhaps today his uncharacteristically prickly mood would have lifted. "And how was your morning walk?"

"Brisk." He rubbed his hands together, blew on them, then reached over and placed one on either side of her face.

Annie jumped backward. "Your hands are freezing!" But she didn't mind since it seemed his usual teasing manner had returned.

He grinned at her. "I thought maybe you'd like to share some of my outdoor experience, especially as you've been laying about inside where it's nice and warm."

She gave him a look of mock indignation. "I wouldn't say I've been laying about. *Somebody* has to see that things are in working order for this upcoming workshop." Then she took a hold of his arm and said in a much lower voice, "I've been hearing more eerie tales about this place."

He looked down at her questioningly. "Eerie?" He thought of the spectacular fall landscape he'd hiked that morning. It had been refreshing, head-clearing, anything but eerie.

She steered him in the direction of the kitchen. "Trilby claims her ex-manager took everything with him but some paintings. Maxine says she moved a lot more than that into the attic."

"Do you think Trilby is carrying on a family tradition?"

"And what would that be?"

"Remember Ben Stokes suggested Elmira Watkins killed people with her so-called cures."

"Don't even suggest such a thing!" But she drew a little closer to him and it was all he could do to keep from taking her in his arms. "And that's not all. I've once again heard the tale of the two women who disappeared while staying here, never to be seen again. I've decided gossip must be in short supply if people are still hashing over that old story."

"Maybe they went into the Witness Protection Program."

Annie frowned at him even though she knew he was kidding. "Was it around then?"

"Don't know. Maybe they just wanted to start a new life—walked out of the old and into the new. People do occasionally."

She glanced up at him alarmed. Was this a forewarning of what he was planning or simply a suggestion? She couldn't stand to consider the thought of him leaving. She tried to keep any hint of panic from her voice. "Yes, well, the strong suggestion is that the new life they walked into was in the next world."

"There's a lot of back country out there. I can see how someone might get lost and stay lost. Anyway, there's your next plot. Solve their disappearance."

She gave his suggestion a moment's thought. "Do you think it possible we could while we're here?" She deliberately included him.

"Haven't others already tried?"

"Undoubtedly—but they weren't us!"

"Sorry, Annie, but I can only deal with one plot at a time."

She tried to hide her disappointment and knew she failed. "Aren't you the least bit curious? Can't I tempt you?"

She tempted him all right, but not in the way she meant. Unless he was going to slip back into the dark mood that had been hounding him, he'd better change the subject. "How's our hostess this morning?"

Annie knew a deliberate change of subject when she heard it. "Unorganized. She keeps telling me she has things in hand, but I've seen very little evidence that she's telling me the truth. Every time something a little unexpected happens she takes on this panicked look." And she regaled him with Fran Shipman's call and Trilby's reaction to the prospect of unexpected guests.

"So you think mail is going astray?"

"Who knows? She could simply have been late in registering and rather than admit the fact, fell back on the overworked excuse that the reservation was in the mail. Although I have to admit I'm surprised the response to the workshops has been so poor."

"I know the low registration isn't what you're used to, but maybe it will pick up."

"I certainly hope so, since the first workshop is the only one with any interest so far. If we don't get more response, this trip won't have been worth our while. And I know this is a tight time for you."

"There was no way I was going to let you come here on your own with Trilby calling you up in the middle of the night insisting someone was trying to kill her. Which seems to have been a figment of her imagination, as far as I can tell. Anyway, I brought my notes and my laptop. While you're conducting the workshops I intend to write. That's why I didn't offer to help out any more than running to the store. If there's food in the cupboards, surely Trilby can put something together. On the positive side, we're getting a change of scene and it's costing us very little." He couldn't resist brushing a wisp of hair away from her cheek. "And maybe you're already cooking up an idea for your next plot."

"Since that's about the only thing I can cook up." Annie knew she was hopeless in the kitchen.

"That's what TV dinners are for."

She squeezed his arm, "And you." She referred to the

fact that he often invited her over to his caretaker's cottage for dinner.

"Oh, believe me, Annie, I'm good for a lot more than that."

Annie swallowed hard and tried to think of how to respond. "I know that."

"How could you when you never give me a chance to prove it? I'm always at arm's length with a hammer in one hand and nails in the other."

Annie blushed and looked away. "I don't mean to take advantage of you. . . ."

"And here I've been hoping."

Annie was thrown off guard. She felt awkward and to cover that feeling returned to a safe subject. "Did you encounter anything of interest while you were out walking?"

"I might have found something." He knew Annie's insatiable curiosity would be tempted and he wanted to move away from discussing a situation he was unsure how to handle. Anyway, this wasn't the time or the place.

Her curiosity was instantly aroused. "What? Did you really find something or are you just being mysterious?"

"I think it would be better if I show you. But later, after I've had some breakfast. All that fresh air has made me hungry. What's on the menu for breakfast?"

"Not much, I'm afraid. Cereal, scones, and coffee."

"You're kidding?"

She shook her head. "I wish I was."

Trilby was no where in sight when they reached the kitchen, but an assortment of cereal boxes and a plate heaped with scones sat on the table. Brendan opened the refrigerator door. "Wonder if there's an egg in the place. Nope, doesn't look like it. Guess I'll have to make do with a helping of grains." Brendan filled a bowl with cereal only to discover there wasn't any milk.

Annie pushed the plate of scones in his direction. "They're quite good." Brendan was a big man, physically active and a substantial eater, so she knew it would take several scones to fill him up. "We can walk down to the Log Cabin Café later. Maybe indulge in a combination late breakfast, early lunch." Her tone was hopeful as she welcomed the thought of getting away for a little while, maybe even trying out Ben Stokes's peach pie.

Brendan spread butter on a scone and took a large bite.

"While you're eating I have something I want to show you." She pushed back her chair. "I'll be right back." She hurried into the lobby, grabbed the drawing pad from under the counter, and returned to the kitchen. "Trilby's late lamented manager left this behind." She turned quickly to the sketch that had captivated her earlier. "Look at this."

"He's good."

"True, but that's not why I'm showing it to you. When you're out walking I want you to keep your eyes open for the original. Apparently this is drawn from real life and I'd like to see it. According to Maxine, this sculpture has almost legendary status. People talk about it, but no one claims to know where it is. It seems to me it's pretty obvious the unaccounted-for manager found it and now we don't know where he is. The two women who disappeared were reportedly looking for this rock carving the day they vanished."

"Interesting."

"Indeed. So will you be on the lookout for her? It won't be any extra time away from your manuscript—just as a part of your regular morning walk."

Brendan held the drawing at arm's length. "Did you notice that while there are trees all around, the area beyond the carving appears to be barren?"

"I did."

He nodded, "I'll be on the lookout for her."

"I know it will be sheer luck if you find it, but . . ."

"But you still want me to try." Then he added with mock seriousness, "Are you hoping I'll vanish also?"

"Don't be ridiculous. What in the world would I do without you?" She didn't wait for an answer. "Maybe I'm jumping to conclusions, but there are too many unusual things going on around here. Somebody needs to get to the bottom of these mysteries, and I intend to be that somebody. Maybe settling these issues once and for all would do more to help Trilby and the resort than the workshops ever could. Because I'm doubtful the writing workshops will do anything more than postpone the inevitable shutdown of the resort. And it's too bad because this really is a lovely place. But Trilby is neglecting most of its potential."

"The hot springs being number one on that list. Do you know if Trilby has done much advertising?"

"We haven't talked specifically about that, but I would assume . . ."

Brendan glanced up and his expression stopped Annie in mid-sentence. It took little imagination to guess Trilby had arrived on the scene.

"Are the two of you getting enough to eat?" Then she stated the obvious. "Sorry I let supplies get so low. I'll get that list ready and give you some money, Brendan, and you can get the shopping done. That is, if your offer still holds."

"It does."

"Okay. Do either of you have any special requests?"

Brendan poured himself more coffee. "That we keep it simple. Like I've already suggested—deli trays, good bread for sandwiches, an assortment of muffins and rolls for breakfast. We can get the latter at the bakery, then all you'll have to worry about is supper. How does that sound?"

"Like you've taken charge, and I love it."

"No, I haven't taken charge. I'm only making a suggestion or two." He wasn't about to let himself get involved any deeper than he already was.

"Well, I do appreciate your suggestions. They would certainly simplify things, and I have to admit I'm feeling a bit overwhelmed by all this."

Brendan finished off the last of his coffee and tried not to grimace. Picking up some decent coffee was going to be high on his list. "You get that list together while I take

Annie out for a walk. She needs some exercise. Come on, Annie, let's give Trilby time to think." He took Annie's hand and pulled her up from the table, not letting go until they were well away from the kitchen. "I want more than cereal without milk and scones for my breakfast. So what do you say we walk in the direction of the Log Cabin Café. I want some real food before I set off to the supermarket, otherwise I'll buy everything in sight. And I doubt Trilby could afford that."

Annie hesitated, knowing there were undoubtedly plenty of things she could or should be doing to help Trilby get ready.

Brendan sensed her hesitation. "I'll treat you to that piece of peach pie you coveted last night."

"You know how awful you are, don't you? Appealing to my weakest side."

"Only because I could almost read your thoughts. You think you should stay around in case Trilby needs you. Well, your part of the deal with her is to put on the work-shops. Hers, to provide food and lodging. You need a break before the guests start to arrive." His gently chiding tone softened and he took hold of her shoulders, turning her to face him, and spoke in an even gentler tone. "Boss Lady, you can't be everything to everybody. Okay?" He deliberately softened his voice to take the sting out of his words.

"I'm not your boss, Brendan. And I wish you wouldn't call me that. It implies a relationship that doesn't exist."

"Is somebody forging your name on my checks, then?" His tone was teasing, but he regretted the remark as soon as he saw the hurt expression on Annie's face.

"If my name on your paychecks is coming between us, then I'll put Harbor House on the market."

"Annie love! That's the last thing I want you to do."

Annie love! She felt her heartbeat accelerate. As soon as she started to speak, she knew her voice had taken on an out-of-breath quality and she swallowed the words she'd been about to say. His endearment made her realize with an ache how much she really did want to be his *Annie love*, and because of that she wandered—for her—clear out on a limb. "I just want you to know that I want nothing to come between us. And I'll do what's necessary to keep something like that from happening."

"Then let's forget about this place for a while at least and head down to the Log Cabin Café for a decent breakfast?"

"How could I possibly refuse?"

"I don't know, but in case you suddenly think of a way, let's get out of here."

Brendan held her hand while leading her down the edge of the driveway, which prompted her to ask, "Are we on the lam?"

"I don't want Trilby asking to join us."

It was the perfect time of day for a walk. The air was deliciously crisp and fresh, free of the chemical smells one accepted as part of life in the city. Not quite the same as the sea smells Annie associated with Harbor House, but equally as refreshing. Born and raised in the city, she was still amazed at how well she'd adapted to the slower pace of life on the coast. They walked along the highway, Annie marveling at the autumn beauty of their surroundings. "It's gorgeous this time of year in the High Cascades."

"Trilby's sitting on an undeveloped gold mine. No doubt about it in my mind."

Annie didn't know what to expect when the Log Cabin Café came into view. Was this an early morning hot spot where they'd have to wait for a place at the counter, or would they have the place to themselves and another chance to gossip with Ben Stokes? There were no cars pulled into the parking spaces, which left her hoping they'd be the only customers. Her hope soon dashed when she noticed an elderly man in the back booth who was so intent on his mug of coffee that he didn't even look up when they entered. Even though the store was warm inside, he wore a heavy red plaid mackinaw and a ski cap pulled down over his ears. With no cars in sight, Annie wondered if he lived nearby—maybe even in one of the attached cabins.

Ben Stokes was polishing the counter and looked up when they pushed open the door. "Well, I wondered when you'd be coming back for that piece of pie—or maybe just some fresh air."

They both slid onto stools, Annie leaning her elbows on the counter. "It certainly is invigorating outside. The landscape is glorious with fall color."

"Yep—it's hard to beat the gold of quaking aspen in the fall." He poured them coffee without asking. "It's fresh—or was five minutes ago."

Annie reached for the cream neatly positioned with salt and pepper shakers, a sugar container, and a napkin holder. Everything was scrupulously clean. "Thanks, it'll be ambrosia if it only tastes half as good as it smells." She glanced back at the elderly man. "Are we ahead or behind the breakfast crowd?"

Stokes shook his head almost regretfully. "Never any crowd. On a good day, a slow trickle. Late summer and hunting season are the best times. Otherwise I'm off the beaten track. I live here because I like it and it's home, not because I'm getting rich."

Annie took a sip of surprisingly good coffee, while Brendan replaced the menu. "I'll have the number one breakfast, eggs over easy."

"Hash browns or toast with that?"

"Hash browns."

"And for you, young lady?"

"Is it too early for a piece of that peach pie?"

"It's never too early for my special pie. Your orders are coming right up."

The kitchen was mostly open and just beyond the counter. Annie only raised her voice a little so Ben could hear her. "When we talked last night you gave us the impression you'd been here a long time."

"Born and raised."

Brendan was letting Annie take the lead in the conversation, but from the corner of his eye he could see the elderly man in the corner suddenly raise his head and look in their direction, interest etched in his expression.

"Then you know most everything that's gone on around here."

"Yeah. . . ."

Annie wondered if Ben Stokes's reticence meant he regretted all the information he'd volunteered the night before or if he was simply inhibited by the presence of someone else in the store. Well, she wasn't going to let that stop her from trying to find out more about Whispering Pines. "What can you tell us about the resort in its heyday?"

He reached into the cooler for pancake batter and eggs. "I'm not that old."

"I didn't mean to imply that you were, but last night you talked quite a bit about the lodge."

"Sometimes I talk too much." And he glanced at the old man in the corner.

"But we're interested—I'm interested. I make my living as a writer and I like to gather local color wherever I go. It adds depth to my stories. Besides, I'm curious as to what *really* closed the resort down. As you say, this area is off the beaten track."

Ben Stokes dropped his voice to the point that she had to lean forward to hear what he was saying. "Elmira, like the current proprietor, had trouble keeping help. And the state began to clamp down on places like Whispering Pines. Began demanding licenses and insurance and regular inspections. Especially after a number of people complained. If Elmira hadn't made any outlandish claims for the therapeutic quality of the waters up there, she might have stayed in business a bit longer. Those hot springs can temporarily soothe aching joints and muscles, but she started claiming that drinking them could cure kidney stones, cancer, even baldness if you washed your hair in them. She tried bottling the waters and that really got her into hot water—no pun intended. People will buy anything, but then they started getting sick and the sickness could be traced to Whispering Pines's Magic Waters. Well, that brought the law to her doorstep. The frosting on the cake were those disappearances."

He placed a heaping platter of pancakes, bacon, eggs, and hash browns in front of Brendan, who wasted no time in tucking in to the welcome array of food. The generous wedge of peach pie he set in front of Annie looked almost meager in comparison.

Brendan poured syrup over his pancakes. "Best breakfast I've had in a long time."

"Buttermilk's the secret. I don't think you can make a decent pancake without it."

Compliments out of the way, Brendan stated the obvious. "There's a lot of back country out there. It wouldn't be all that hard to get lost."

"That's true, it happens frequently with hunters. But they always find some trace of them or what happened to them. That's not the case with those two women who were staying at the resort and supposedly wandered off."

Annie thought for someone who didn't claim to be that old, Ben Stokes was remembering a lot of details now that he'd overcome his initial hesitation. But she said nothing lest it stem the flow of information.

"There wasn't a shred of evidence or proof that they ever left the resort property. Which gave rise to a lot of gossip that in fact they hadn't. That Elmira's magic cure had cured what ailed them—permanently. And that she gave out the story they were lost in the woods to cover any liability on her part."

"I've heard from the housekeeper that they were looking for the rock carving of a Native American woman when they disappeared."

"Maxine is a hard worker and everybody around here admires the way she's raising those five kids all on her own. But let's face it. She's not about to bite the hand that's feeding her and her kids. Work's too hard to come by around here."

"So you don't think the rock carving exists?"

"Let's put it this way. I've never known a soul who's actually seen it."

Annie was reluctant to let the subject go entirely. "But stories like that usually have some basis to get started."

"Yeah, in somebody's imagination. You find that rock carving, show it to me personally, and then I'll believe it exists and in the possibility those two women disappeared trying to find it. And not that they're buried somewhere in the woods behind the resort, victims of one of Elmira Watkins's miracle cures."

Brendan swiped a last bite of pancake through the syrup remaining on his plate and recalled what he'd found that morning in a shaded glen behind the resort. He had yet to show it to Annie, but wondered at the possibilities it called into being.

"Surely the authorities searched for them."

"The search went on for weeks, but they never found a thing. Nothing."

"Was it possible the women checked out without telling anyone?"

"They left everything behind that they'd brought with them. So that possibility didn't seem likely then or now."

Aware Stokes was a source of information, Annie decided to ask if he had ever seen the strange flashing lights in the night sky that had startled her the previous night. "Tell me, Ben, have you or anyone you know seen flashing lights in the night sky?"

He frowned and looked away. "People around here have learned to ignore them."

"Why? I'd think people would be curious and would want to know what caused them."

She was waiting for Ben Stokes's answer when she felt someone come up behind her. Turning slightly she recognized the elderly man who'd been keeping the corner booth warm.

"Young lady, didn't anybody ever tell you that curiosity killed the cat and that some things are better left alone? You ask too many questions about too many things that have nothin' to do with you. If you're smart, you'll stay out of those woods. People *have* disappeared in that back country and there's nothin' to stop it from happenin' again." He didn't wait for her to recover and answer but strode from the cafe, letting the door bang shut behind him.

Chapter Six

Annie glanced from Brendan to Ben. "I don't know if I've just been threatened or warned. Maybe a little bit of both." Not bothering to hide her surprise, she turned back to Stokes. "He was eavesdropping on our conversation."

"Why do you think I dropped my voice? I could tell he was straining to hear."

"But why? Why should he care what we were talking about?"

"Nothing better to do, I guess."

Perhaps Ben Stokes was right, but Annie wondered why a stranger would be that interested in what they'd had to say. And beyond that, why would he reveal he'd been eavesdropping by butting into a personal conversation.

Brendan didn't think the man's interest was due to lack of anything else to do. While Annie pumped Ben Stokes for information he had enjoyed his breakfast, at the same time keeping an eye on the changes of awareness and interest taking place in the back booth. "What do you know about him, Ben? Anything? There weren't any cars outside so he must live near here."

"I haven't a clue. He comes in here almost every day for coffee, and every Monday regular as clockwork he buys some groceries. A package of baloney, can of evaporated milk, pork and beans, cold cereal. Stuff you don't have to cook."

Brendan barely suppressed a shudder at the thought of living on such fare, but he knew they were cheap items that would quell hunger pangs if not exactly satisfy the palate. "How long's he been coming in?"

"About four or five months now. I don't know anything more about him than I did after the first time he came in here. I've tried getting him to talk, but what you just heard him say is longer than any conversation I've had with him. The guy's a real clam."

"Did you ever ask him where he was staying?"

"Sure I did, and he told me he moved around a lot. I can take a hint and know when I'm being told to mind my own business. Besides, I'm not about to drive a regular customer away. There aren't that many of them." Then, as if moved by the disappointed look he saw on Annie's face, he added, "If I were to make a guess, I'd say he was camping out."

This intrigued Brendan. "You mean he's living in the woods around here?"

Stokes nodded. "It's not unusual for someone otherwise homeless to camp out until the cold weather sets in. There are plenty of lava caves for shelter if you don't have any-where else to go. And I'd say from the looks of him that he doesn't have much."

Brendan turned on his stool to look back toward the door. "Hmm, it's apt to get mighty cold soon. Since he walks here, he can't be camped too far away." It was just a thought, but he recalled Trilby claiming that food went missing from the resort. Could the old guy have discovered some way in and be supplementing his meager rations with a little home cooking? It was a possibility worth investigating. He slid off the stool. "Look, Annie, you hang around if you want. I'm going to head back."

Annie knew what Brendan intended and she didn't think Ben Stokes had any more to tell her. "I'll come with you. I think I've avoided my responsibilities long enough."

She waited while Brendan paid their bill and then they walked outside together. The older man had a good head start and was evidently in fit condition because he was only a dot on the road.

"He's really moving along," Annie said.

"And I want to catch up and see where he's headed."

"Brendan, are you going to try and talk to him?"

"I don't intend to let him know I'm following if I can help it."

"Why?"

"Remember Trilby claimed food and small items were missing from the lodge?"

"Yes. . . ."

"Well, maybe we've just met the culprit."

"But how would he get in?"

"There are ways if a person is determined enough. Anyway, it's just a hunch but one I want to follow up on."

"Why exactly?"

"Annie, he wouldn't have given you a warning if he didn't have some idea what was going on."

"With the lights?"

"With everything we were talking about."

"And you're going to follow him?"

"I am."

"What about whatever it was you found this morning and were going to show me?" Annie asked.

"I'll still show it to you. But what I found isn't going anywhere and this guy is. Come on, I don't want to lose him altogether."

Brendan set a good pace and she was almost breathless trying to keep up. "I don't understand why you think he might be taking things from the lodge."

"It's just a feeling based on his warning to you and the interest he was showing in our conversation. Ben Stokes might not recognize him, but I'd be willing to bet money he's no stranger to this area."

"Do you think he's someone who might have stayed at the resort at one time?"

"Maybe—I don't know for sure what I'll find out, but I intend to at least discover where he's living."

Brendan wasn't at all surprised when the man disappeared from the main road at the turnoff to the resort.

But Annie was. "He's headed for the lodge."

"I know it looks that way, but I'll bet it's not his destination."

Sure enough, when they reached the bend in the road that heralded the last few hundred feet before reaching the parking lot of the lodge there was a faint trail leading into the woods. One easily missed if you weren't looking for it. Brendan turned to Annie. "Are you game to follow him?"

"I'd like nothing better, but truly, I don't dare spend any more time away. I want to make certain Trilby has her shopping list ready and that there aren't going to be any last-minute surprises. Don't forget in your enthusiasm to play the tracker that you promised to go to the store."

"I haven't and I won't. I don't imagine I'll have to go far to discover where he's staying."

Annie watched with reluctance as Brendan walked uphill into the timber. She lost sight of him when he ducked under the branches of a quaking aspen and a shower of gold was all the evidence he'd passed that way.

Brendan knew Annie wanted to accompany him, but he didn't want to miss this opportunity. He didn't know if he could locate where the man was camping or if he could do it without being seen. But it was certainly worth a try. The trail was faint, in places almost nonexistent, but he followed the obvious natural bends around trees and fallen logs. The path led uphill, the trees and brush thinning out considerably as he climbed. He'd just begun to wonder if he'd lost his quarry when he came upon a pristine lake. He stepped back quickly into the trees when he saw the object of his pursuit on the other side pulling a canoe up onto the shore. Brendan realized he'd gone as far as he could for the moment. He could walk around the perimeter of the lake and reach the other side that way. But by the time he reached the canoe he would have lost all possibility of seeing which direction the man had gone. And there wasn't time now for such a trek. But there was always tomorrow. He'd bet anything the elderly man was no stranger to lights in the night sky or two women missing almost fifty years.

Chapter Seven

As Annie approached the lodge she tried to quell feelings of disappointment that she couldn't accompany Brendan on his manhunt. Like him, she was curious about the man who had eavesdropped on their conversation with Ben Stokes. He'd threatened her, which had to mean he knew something about the events puzzling her.

Her musings on the past and its possible connection with the present were immediately shelved when she noticed a car in the parking lot. Workshop participants weren't due to start arriving until tomorrow.

Annie pushed open the heavy front door of the lodge to find a gray-haired woman meandering around the lobby. Annie watched with some amusement as she ran a gloved finger over the fireplace mantel and then tried out first one and then the other of the leather chairs.

Annie was about to say something when the woman turned and saw her. "Well, I must say I wondered if anybody was around. No cars in the parking lot and no staff on duty at the desk. I'm Louella Haven, by the way." She extended a hand clad in black cotton dress gloves shiny with age.

Annie shook hands and in turn introduced herself. "I'm Annie Kirk." She had thought Louella Haven, the seventy-five-year-old who knew she had at least one good book in her, sounded like fun when she'd read her registration form. Actually meeting her underscored that first impression. It had been a long time since she'd encountered anyone wearing dress gloves and a navy blue straw hat complete with drooping cherries—artificial, of course. The woman made a charming picture.

Louella hastened to explain. "I know I'm early. I haven't had my driver's license very long and I never know how much time it's going to take me to get places. You know how that is. Things always look so deceptively close together on a map. I was afraid for a few minutes that I had beaten everyone here—including the staff."

"The lodge is reserved exclusively for the workshop and so the staff are busy and probably didn't hear you come in." No need to mention the staff consisted of the owner and one housekeeper. "I myself have been out for a walk. Enjoying leisure time while I can."

"Is my early arrival going to be a problem? I can probably find accommodations elsewhere."

"Nonsense, of course you won't do that. If you don't mind that everything isn't quite in place, then we don't mind that you're early."

Louella Haven nodded and looked around appraisingly. "Well, well. This is quite the place. Yes, indeed. And I didn't have a bit of trouble finding it. Although I would recommend a sign down by the highway. Not everyone has my sense of direction. No indeed." And she straightened the straw hat that perched precariously on her salt-and-pepper curls. A knee-length brown coat, sensible walking shoes, and heavy stockings completed her ensemble.

Annie couldn't help smiling at the woman who she would bet brought enthusiasm to everything she did. "Actually, your being a bit ahead of the others will give us a chance to get acquainted. Here." She picked up the small suitcase that seemed to be all the woman had brought with her. "I'll help you get your things to your room." Although until she found Trilby, she wasn't quite sure which room that would be. Aware also of the emptiness of Trilby's pantry and that all workshop participants had been told there would be meals on site, Annie was wondering what she could offer Louella in the way of refreshment.

"As I mentioned, we're not completely organized and I need to check with the resort owner on room assignments. So could I offer you a cup of tea or coffee and perhaps a scone while I locate her and find out which room you're in?"

"Oh, tea and a scone would be delightful."

"I can either bring it to you out here or you can take it in the kitchen. Whichever you'd prefer."

"Oh, the kitchen is fine. I don't want to put you out any more than I probably am already."

"No problem, don't worry."

Louella sat down at the round pine table, adjusted her glasses, and took further notice of her surroundings, almost as if she was cataloging them. "This is quite a place. Has it been here a long time?"

Annie put water on to heat. "I'm not actually sure when it was built, but I do know it was operating as a health spa as far back as the 1940's." She was just pouring Louella a cup of tea when Brendan came in through the back door.

"I thought someone must have arrived."

"Brendan, this is Louella Haven. Louella, this is Brendan Marshall."

Louella extended her hand, now minus the worn cotton glove. "I'm always pleased to meet a good-looking man."

Brendan laughed. "And I'm always pleased to meet an attractive woman."

"Young man, you'll turn my head if you aren't careful. Are you taking the workshop also?"

"No, I'm a good friend of Annie's, just along for the ride."

Brendan's success with people always pleased Annie. "Brendan is also a writer—although he concentrates on non-fiction." Turning her attention to Brendan, she said, "We really need to get that shopping list from Trilby so you can be on your way." Then, in an aside she hoped only he could hear, "It's a bit embarrassing to have nothing more than scones to offer."

"Gotcha—I'll see if I can locate Trilby or the list."

There was a blackboard on the wall beside the door and Trilby had listed a few necessities on it. Brendan had noticed it the night before and it hadn't been updated since, except that someone had scrawled *Go away!!!!* across the bottom. He glanced over his shoulder, and when he saw that no one was paying any attention to him, he erased it. Was this an example of Trilby's threats? He'd mention it to Annie later.

There was only a partial list of groceries on the kitchen counter, but he knew from a previous glance into the pantry that it was nowhere near complete. Hearing the distant sound of Maxine's vacuum he headed in that direction. Perhaps the housekeeper knew where Trilby was.

Maxine was just carrying a bucket of cleaning supplies into a bathroom when he caught up with her. "Maxine, can you give me a minute?"

The housekeeper was more than willing to stop work and chat with the good lookin' guy Miz Watkins's friend had brought with her. "What can I do for you?"

"I'm looking for Trilby. Have you seen her?"

"About twenty minutes ago. She was headed up to the third floor. Up where the spook room is."

"Spook room? What are you talking about?"

Maxine popped her gum and gave him an impish look. "I don't know what else you'd call it. It's the room where Elmira Watkins used to talk with the dead. Or try to anyway."

Brendan couldn't help being curious. "Who was Elmira trying to contact?"

Maxine rocked back and forth from the balls of her feet

to her heels, all the while cracking her gum. "Her oldest son, Wilbur Watkins."

Brendan instantly associated the name with the find he'd made earlier that morning. A discovery he had yet to share with Annie.

"Old Elmira never did accept the fact of Wilbur's death. He was shot down over in Europe during World War II, but Elmira never believed he was really dead. She kept expecting him to walk through the door any old day."

Maxine wasn't nearly old enough to know what Elmira Watkins had done or thought, except by hearsay. "Isn't that a contradiction? You try to contact someone who is supposed to be dead because you believe they're still alive?"

Maxine shrugged. "Hey, I never said it made sense. But if you want Miz Watkins that's where she is—upstairs in the spook room. Door's at the end of the third floor hall." And she returned to her cleaning duties.

The door Maxine had indicated opened onto a flight of wooden stairs. Brendan took them two at a time and found himself in a mostly unfurnished attic. Sunlight streamed through windows at either end of the large room that extended the length of the lodge. There were a few boxes, but not much else that he could see. Had Maxine sent him on a fool's errand?

"Trilby? Are you up here?"

"Over here, Brendan."

He turned to find her standing in a section of wall that had slid away to reveal a low, darkened room. "What in the world?"

"Care to have a look?" And she stood aside to allow him room to enter. "It was Elmira Watkins's séance room."

What was Trilby doing poking around in the attic when there was work to be done? "Guests have started arriving, so I thought I'd better get to the grocery store. Do you have a finished list?"

"I started making one. When I went to copy the items from the chalkboard I saw something I hadn't written."

Trilby seemed about to choke on the fear in her voice. "I don't know why, but I feel safe in this room."

"I saw the warning, Trilby, and I erased it. I didn't think either Annie or our first arrival needed to see it."

"Someone is here already?" Alarm replaced her fear.

"That's what I just said. So I need to get to the store. Is there any list other than the one I saw on the kitchen counter?"

"No, I'll get busy and finish it." She glanced with reluctance at the small, dark room behind her.

Brendan let Trilby lead the way downstairs. That way he knew he wouldn't lose her. When they reached the kitchen, Annie and Louella Haven were enjoying a cup of tea, a scone, and from the sound of things, a good chat. Annie looked relieved to see Trilby. "Trilby, this is Louella Haven. I didn't know if you had made room assignments yet so I wasn't sure where to put her."

Trilby suddenly became a bit more businesslike. "All the rooms are the same size, so I thought we could start at one end and work toward the other." She reached for her unfinished shopping list and began scribbling madly.

"Then we'll finish our tea and I'll get her settled in."

"Annie, could I talk to you for a minute?"

"Certainly, Brendan, what's up?" Annie turned to Louella. "I'll be right back."

"Oh, no hurry. I'll just have another one of these delicious scones and some more hot water. Take your time. I know I'm early."

Brendan and Annie stepped out into the hall. "Is something wrong?"

"Just so you know, there was a warning scrawled on the kitchen blackboard. It turns out Trilby had already seen it and taken refuge in what she calls Elmira's séance room."

Annie shook her head. "At least Louella didn't see it. What did it say?"

"Go away!!!!"

"Not exactly a death threat, but certainly undermining if

part of a series. Who could possibly have left it? I haven't seen anyone else around except Maxine and I doubt it's her. She needs this job."

"I agree, but at least we know there really are warnings."

"Brendan, you don't think Trilby could have written it herself?"

"To win our sympathy?"

"To prove they're really happening. She's talked about them, but this is the first one either you or I have seen."

He shrugged. "Who knows—it's possible I suppose. And could be why she's reluctant to call in the police."

Annie took hold of Brendan's arm and pulled him farther into the hallway and away from what she suspected were Louella Haven's perked ears. It was obvious from the very beginning that Louella missed nothing. "Brendan, I'm really sorry. I had no idea the state Trilby was in or I would never have agreed to come."

"Annie, you and I both know that isn't true. Somebody cries help and you run to the rescue. I've seen you do it time and again. Have you forgotten Alistair McDougal and his mystery game?"

"Well, I shouldn't have let you come with me. I know and appreciate the deadline you're under."

"I wasn't about to let you come alone, given the circumstances. We're here now and so we'll just have to make the best of it. Meanwhile, see if you can light a fire under Trilby while I'm gone. She should at least look alert and glad to see guests, and not like something that's blown in on a dust cloud."

Annie rushed to the defense of her old college friend. "We know she's financially strapped and recently widowed. Maybe everything is just too much for her right now."

"Well, her ineptitude is too much for me. I'd better get going."

Annie didn't have a chance to talk with Trilby until after Louella Haven was settled in her room. Several cups of tea later, Louella finally announced, "I'll just take a rest now if you don't mind. Then maybe a walk later. I do enjoy wandering about in nature."

Annie felt a sudden premonition of possible disaster. Louella Haven was maybe all of four-foot-ten and with her hat and gloves didn't look a likely candidate for a tromp in the woods. Still, she couldn't demand the older woman stay indoors. "You might want to be careful not to wander too far from the lodge. Perhaps it would be a good idea to let one of us know before you set out. Maybe even see if we'd be able to go with you."

"Pooh, don't worry about me. I have an excellent sense of direction. And I'm a good walker. Remember I only recently got my driver's license. These feet of mine got me from point A to point B countless times."

Annie had taken an instant liking to the older woman who was delighted with her room and asked eager, insightful questions concerning the workshop. She couldn't help hoping that all the participants would be as charming as their earliest arrival. After getting her settled, Annie went into her own room and set about organizing some of her workshop materials. Then, remembering her promise to Brendan, she went in search of Trilby. A search that was circumvented when she glanced out the window and caught sight of the elderly man from the Log Cabin Café crossing into the trees. Without giving herself time to reconsider, Annie went in pursuit.

The man had only the briefest of head starts, but he was gone before she got outside. She knew the direction he'd taken previously and so she headed that way. She had no idea how far she'd walked when she had to rest a minute and get her second wind. The older man seemed to know these woods like the back of his hand. There was no sense going any deeper into the timber when she had no idea which way to go.

Disgruntled and disappointed, Annie returned to the lodge, grateful at least that she hadn't gotten herself lost. She heard a car door slam, and thinking it might be Brendan and that he would need help with the groceries, she went around to the front of the lodge. But it wasn't Brendan, it was Louella, and she was engrossed in reading a sheet of paper she'd taken from her car. When she looked up and saw Annie she quickly stuffed it into her pocket, which Annie thought a little strange. But before she could say anything, Brendan did drive up and there was plenty to keep them both busy, and Louella too if they'd accepted her offer of help.

When everything was finally put away, Brendan turned to Annie and said, "Now I want to show you what I found this morning. It'll really fuel your imagination."

"Is it something important?"

"It's interesting. I don't know how important it is."

"Oh, and Brendan, I saw that elderly man again, the one from this morning. He was cutting across the back of the property and I tried to follow him, but with no luck. He knows where he's going and he goes there in a hurry. Did you have any better luck following him?"

"I gave up at the lake. He took the only canoe—probably his own—and I was stranded on shore. I intend to work my way around the lake one of these mornings and see what I can find. But at this point, he's still a mystery. Now, do you want to see what I found or not?"

"Of course I do. Lead the way and I'll follow."

Lead the way and I'll follow. He liked the sound of that because it implied confidence and trust.

Like fountains of gold, aspen showered sprays of fall color amongst the Ponderosa pines. Annie pulled clean air into her lungs. "It is so beautiful up here. There should be standing room only to stay at the lodge."

"True, but Trilby's got to convey the feeling she's doing a little more than just hanging on. If she behaves around guests the way she has around us, they're not going to come back. Or stay long once they've arrived."

"I think she's tried. . . ."

"She has yet to convince me."

Annie found it difficult to defend Trilby, since Trilby was doing so little to promote herself or her project. At the moment, she'd rather focus on Brendan and these moments together. "Where's your big discovery?"

"Not far. There's a trail leading into the woods behind the lodge. What I found is a short walk down that trail."

"Aren't you going to give me any hints?"

"No. It will have more impact if you don't know what to expect."

They followed the dusty path as it wound into the timber. Brown pine needles carpeted the forest floor among pools of fallen aspen leaves. Annie caught a fleeting glimpse of what looked like buildings, but she couldn't be certain. Were they headed in the direction of the abandoned bath-houses? "What am I seeing through the trees?"

"What's left of the bathhouses. Which isn't much."

"Let's have a look at them after I see what you've discovered."

"It's not far now."

A golden mantled ground squirrel darted across the path, and a Clark's nutcracker screeched raucously at them as they stepped into a natural clearing, where tall Ponderosa pines formed a ragged circle. A sudden breeze shuddered through the pines, sending a shower of umber-colored needles drifting downward. They settled in a thin layer over a tell-tale mound crowned with a weathered marker. Annie turned in surprise toward Brendan. "It's a grave!"

Chapter Eight

Brendan nodded in agreement. "That would be my first guess. And notice it appears recently disturbed."

"You don't seriously believe that, do you?" Annie was incredulous.

"Look how mounded the site is. The headstone looks like it's been here a while, therefore the earth should have settled into place by now. But it hasn't, so I would say somebody has been digging here lately."

The thought was appalling to Annie. "Maybe an animal?"

"Not with everything put neatly back in place."

Despite the peacefulness of the sun-dappled glade, Annie felt a sense of unease. The headstone was split in several places and bright green moss crept out of the cracks. She traced the deeply etched letters with her finger.

" 'Wilbur Watkins, beloved son.' "

Brendan watched as she knelt, the sun highlighting copper strands in her hair. "Notice the absence of any dates."

Annie stood up, wiping her hands on her jeans. "You're right. Why do you suppose that is?"

"Your guess is as good as mine. But it does open the door to speculation."

The grove was quiet now, the breeze still. Nevertheless,

Annie rubbed her arms which were covered with goose bumps, even though she wore a heavy sweater and sunlight filtered through the trees. "This is a melancholy place." And she moved closer to Brendan.

"Grave sites have a tendency to encourage that feeling. Even if we'd never heard a ghost story, I bet we'd find graveyards unsettling. But I didn't intend for it to disturb you. I thought you would find it interesting, and the absence of dates curious."

"I do—and it is. I wonder if Trilby can tell us anything about this grave."

"She surely knows about it."

"Who do you suppose Wilbur Watkins is—was?"

"Elmira's son who was presumably shot down during World War II, although his body was never reported found."

Annie looked at him in surprise. "Where did you pick up that piece of information?"

"From Maxine, that inexhaustible fountain of information."

She rubbed her arms again. "For all its beauty, this is a creepy place. When the wind rushes through the aspen leaves it sounds like old bones rattling. I'll be honest with you, Brendan, I'm really surprised to find Trilby living here by herself. I'm not so sure I'd like it. When we were in school together, she'd miss a meal rather than eat by herself. She wouldn't even go shopping alone. She'd been orphaned young and never really felt like she belonged anywhere." Annie again felt a shivering sense of unease coupled with a need to move on. "Let's take a look at those bathhouses."

They stepped into a clearing characterized by tumbledown shacks and a pervasive odor that had Annie wrinkling her nose. "What *is* that smell?"

"The hot springs. It's the minerals, especially the sulfur in them that gives off that rotten-egg smell. But soaking in them does so much for the body that it becomes easy to overlook the aroma. Or so I've read."

Annie walked around the rocky edges of several small springs and peeked inside a sagging building that housed a good-sized pool large enough to swim laps in. "We'll have to try the waters. Isn't that what they always say in period novels?"

"Trilby has a small gold mine here and she's a fool not to make the most of it. She could have all this debris cleared away and let people bathe in the open. Then she could have someone on staff who does massages."

Annie nodded in agreement. "Perhaps we can encourage her in that direction."

"Somehow I doubt it."

"We can at least try. And we've got to try getting to the bottom of these threats she's receiving."

"Let's hope she's not also the sender."

"I can't believe she'd do that." Annie reached down and dipped her fingers in the warm, slightly bubbling water of the nearest spring. "Although I've begun to wonder if the threats aren't more taunting than actually dangerous."

"You think someone just wants to get under her skin in the hopes they can drive her away without taking any action?"

"Exactly."

Brendan nodded. "You might be right, especially if the person responsible has actually met Trilby. Five minutes in her company and you'd know it wouldn't take much to upset her. She jumps at the sound of her own heartbeat."

"Brendan, she's not that bad." Annie defended Trilby out of loyalty, but she knew he was right. "I suppose we should be getting back." She was surprised at her own reluctance to return to the lodge. She hesitated as something half-buried in the dirt caught her eye. She bent down to scrape at it with her fingernail, eventually unearthing a delicate necklace. "Look at this." And she dangled the tarnished chain from her fingers. A tiny reddish stone hung like a teardrop. "Do you suppose this is just costume jewelry or the real thing?"

Brendan rubbed the stone between his thumb and fore-finger. "Precious gems aren't exactly in my line of exper-tise."

Annie tucked it into her pocket. "Nor mine, but I'll take it in to Trilby." She looked around further. "This almost looks like a one-time garbage dump."

"I agree." Rusted and charred tin cans lay scattered about, some half buried in the dirt as the necklace had been and others simply discarded. "But these could have been left by campers. These hot springs must be mighty tempting to people camping out."

A branch snapped behind them and they both turned, expecting to find that Trilby had come in search of them. Annie saw no one and grinned before explaining, "I'm not quite used to forest sounds yet. Maybe we'd better be get-ting back to the lodge."

Brendan hesitated. Annie hadn't glanced up in time to catch the glimpse of red that warned him of someone watching them from the trees. He thought of sending her back to the lodge while claiming he wanted to go for a walk, but he suspected she would insist on accompanying him.

When they got back to the lodge, they found Trilby and Louella in the kitchen. Trilby was sobbing and Louella was trying to comfort her. Annie hurried over to her friend and knelt beside her chair. "What's wrong?"

Trilby could utter nothing but hiccupping sobs so Louella tried to explain. "I was helping Trilby with some baking—I can't sit around doing nothing for long. Some-thing seemed to hit the front door and she went to inves-tigate. I don't know what it was or what upset her, but she's been sobbing like this for several minutes."

"I'll go investigate." Brendan was glad to leave the con-soling to the women. Whatever he'd expected to find, it wasn't the words scrawled in chalk on the porch floor immediately opposite the lodge front doors. *Get out of here! This place doesn't belong to you. Get out or you'll wish you had!!! Trespassers should be shot!*

He returned to the kitchen and gestured to Annie. "Come with me for a minute."

Annie frowned but followed him. "Good grief!"

"Trilby has to report this to the police. Even if it's just malicious mischief, it needs to be stopped."

"Something like this would make me so angry I'd be on the phone to the authorities so fast your head would swim."

"That's what any sensible person would do."

"I think life has overwhelmed Trilby and she can't deal with the possibility of coping with all the issues a police investigation might raise."

"Nevertheless, we're here to offer moral support, so why don't you have a talk with her. I'll take Louella for a walk and you see if you can persuade Trilby to report these threats."

Annie nodded in agreement. "First I want to find Maxine and ask her to clean the porch off. I think it's just written in chalk. We don't want anyone else seeing this. Imagine the impression it would make if anyone else coming for the workshop saw it. I'll be back in a minute." When she returned to the kitchen it was to find Brendan charming Louella, who declared she was quite keen on taking a walk with a handsome younger man. Once they were out of the way, Annie sat down opposite Trilby.

Trilby sniffed and again wiped at her eyes with a soggy Kleenex. "These warnings started about three months ago. That's also when I began to notice food missing and that someone was getting into the lodge at night."

"But why would anyone accuse you of trespassing?"

Trilby blew her nose. "I—I don't know. Maybe somebody who hates me."

"Somebody who hates you. Now why in the world would anyone around here hate you?"

"I don't know who or why—unless maybe it's Ben

Stokes. That and the warning on the chalkboard are the first messages I've seen in two weeks and I thought maybe they'd stopped. For a while they were showing up every day and I think that's partly why I've had trouble keeping housekeepers."

"You've kept Maxine."

"Maxine has five kids to feed. She's desperate and there's no work around here."

"Trilby, you need to report these threats, warnings, whatever you want to call them, to the police."

Trilby shook her head emphatically. "No—no, I don't want the police up here poking around and asking me questions I can't answer. I want nothing to do with them. Besides, can't you just imagine what the locals would say?"

"You'd rather be harassed into a nervous breakdown?"

"I'm not that bad off."

"I disagree. You're too thin, too nervous, and so overwhelmed you can't settle down to one task and finish it before you wander off to another. I know you've been having some problems—that things haven't been easy for you, losing your job and your husband. But Trilby, heartless as it may sound, life does go on and you have the perfect opportunity with this lodge for a new start. But I don't get the feeling you even care. I came here as a favor to you. The workshops were your idea, but I'm beginning to get the impression that your heart isn't in them any more than it is in reopening this resort. So why are you even here? Why struggle with finances, lack of help, and threats if it really doesn't matter to you?"

Trilby ran her hands through her already disheveled hair. "I really do want to reopen the resort. Honestly, I do. But there's just so much going on. . . ." And her voice dwindled off.

Annie resisted the urge to shake her. "Trilby, if you think there's a lot going on now, wait until all the guests arrive. You have no idea how demanding some people can be. They're going to want coffee, tea, water, and they're going to want to be fed. In fact they're going to expect it because it was advertised as part of the package. And they're going to want all of it immediately if not sooner."

Trilby looked at her with eyes awash in tears. The floodgates looked about to open once again and Annie tried to circumvent them. "You mentioned earlier that you think Ben Stokes might be behind the threats you've received. What makes you think that?"

"It's a long story. . . ."

"I'm prepared to listen."

"And I'm not at all certain it is Stokes. I just can't think of anyone else." She hesitated and Annie grew impatient.

"I'm waiting, Trilby."

"I'm just not sure where to begin. . . ."

"At the beginning is always a safe bet."

Trilby sighed deeply. "Annie, I *do not* believe in ghosts. And yet . . ."

"And yet what?"

"And yet, ever since I got here there have been things going on that I can't explain."

Annie thought of the strange lights she'd seen in the night sky as they drove up to the lodge. "Care to elaborate?"

"I know you talked with Ben Stokes last night and that you've visited with Maxine. Knowing both of them as I do, I can well imagine some of the things they must have told you. They're born gossips, both of them." She hesitated, perhaps wanting Annie to confirm her opinion.

"Quite honestly, most of what they've said pertains to Elmira Watkins and the fact that people around here thought she was a bit crazy. They've both mentioned that she tried to speak with the dead. At first I didn't want to believe it. . . ." She waited for Trilby to say something, perhaps to explain why Brendan had recently found her in the séance room. But Trilby said nothing. Surely Trilby must realize Brendan would have told her.

"Trilby, did Elmira really try to contact the dead?"

"So I've been told."

The very thought made Annie apprehensive. She might profess that she didn't believe in ghosts, but at the same time she would never think of sitting around a table in the dark and inviting the dead in. Just in case they *were* lurking at the door waiting for an invitation to enter.

Trilby closed her eyes and repeated what she'd been told. "Brad's grandfather had a brother who supposedly died during World War II—shot down over the Sea of Denmark. His body was never found, or if it was, it was never properly identified. Therefore Elmira never accepted his death."

"I suppose that's understandable."

"She claims she saw him while she was standing at the kitchen sink—that he was parachuting down from the burning plane and that he said to her, 'Mom, I'm all right.' She claims it was as clear as if he'd been in the room with her. Therefore she never believed he was gone." Trilby managed a half-hearted chuckle at odds with the story she'd just recited. "According to Brad, Elmira was quite a character. Part of the reason Ben Stokes is so grumpy about her is because one time, when he was just a kid, he and some cronies sneaked onto the property with the intention of skinny-dipping in the hot springs. Apparently Elmira never wasted much time sleeping and she chased them off with a shotgun. Trespassing had been Ben's idea and he felt she made him look foolish. So he's never lost an opportunity to bad-mouth her."

"And that's why you think he might be behind the warnings?"

Trilby nodded.

"It seems like a pretty thin reason to harass you, but who knows. Some people will go to great lengths to get even. Tell me, if Elmira didn't really believe her son was dead, why is there a grave and headstone with his name on it in the woods behind the lodge?"

"Oh, you've seen that, have you?" Annie nodded and Trilby continued. "I suppose I should have mentioned it to you so it wouldn't come as a surprise. It's a memorial to Wilbur. Her way of paying tribute and making certain he wasn't forgotten. It was hard for her, never knowing for sure what had happened to him. I understand his fate became an obsession with her."

Annie nodded. "Not knowing what had happened to someone you cared about would be even worse than losing them. You'd always wonder if they were out there somewhere needing you." It wasn't something Annie cared to experience firsthand.

"Exactly, and I think that's why she turned to spiritualism. It was in the hope that there really was something out there, and that her son, if he were indeed dead, would break through the barriers and contact her."

"How old would he be if he *were* still alive?"

"Absolutely ancient."

"Not necessarily—let's do the math."

"Okay, I understand he ran off to enlist when he was seventeen and so he'd be in his late seventies or early eighties. But if he really did survive the plane crash, why didn't he come home?"

"Good question. Amnesia maybe."

Trilby visibly trembled. "You don't think he's really still alive, do you?"

"It doesn't seem likely, but he would be the only logical person with a claim to this property. That is, *if* the person threatening you has a legitimate claim. This could just be some kook with too much time on his hands or somebody who likes to frighten women living alone. There's plenty of those creeps out there."

"But how are they getting into the lodge?"

"Don't you suppose, Trilby, that over the years a good many keys have gone missing?"

"No doubt that's true. But let's return to the possibility of Wilbur Watkins still being alive. Why didn't he come home long ago? And why would he skulk around behind absurd threats rather than walking up to the front door and introducing himself?"

"Which is the best argument I can think of for Wilbur Watkins *not* being the person harassing you. Anyway, you really should go to the police."

Trilby shook her head emphatically. "No, I can't do that."

"Then the threats will undoubtedly continue. Can you live with that? Or the possibility that the person behind them means business and will eventually make good on their threats?"

"Annie, you write mysteries. Don't you think you could solve this one?"

How many times had she heard that argument? "Trilby, I solve mysteries *I* create. That's not quite the same thing."

"No, I suppose not. Speaking of mysteries, our discovery of Big Al's sketchbook and your interest in the rock carving has triggered a remembrance of something I'd forgotten."

Annie sighed inwardly. Once again Trilby had closed the door on dealing effectively with reality.

"Brad liked to read to me in the evenings. One time when we were here, seated in those big leather chairs before a roaring fire, he read from the journal of this woman who explored the back country of Oregon on horseback. He just read me a very small portion of her narrative, but I recall her mentioning a rock carving which she identified as an Indian maiden. She tried to track down its origin. Apparently this isn't a naturally occurring image, but man-made. So who was the sculptor? It seemed no one could tell her, although one person would direct her to another and that person to another. Finally she connected with an elderly Paiute woman, who claimed the sculpture had been there always. That the stone maiden guards sacred ground."

"Do you know where this book might be?"

"Not off hand, but I'll try to find it. It's probably packed away in the attic."

Annie was fascinated. "If the site is accessible by

horseback it must be accessible on foot. And Big Al's sketch is as close to proof as we've got that she's still out there. That time hasn't obliterated her."

"Unless he'd somehow heard about the carving and simply sketched what he thought it might look like."

"There's always that possibility, I suppose. If only we knew where he'd gone. Then we could ask him. You're sure he didn't leave some clue where he was headed?"

Trilby shook her head. "Positive—and believe me, I looked."

"Perhaps he left a note and something happened to it."

"What? What could have happened to it?"

"You've mentioned that things have gone missing."

"Who would want to take a farewell note from my manager? It wouldn't make any sense."

"It might if it was the person leaving the warnings. It would be a little thing, but it would have you wondering what happened to him."

"I suppose you could be right. Even though I'm careful to lock up at night, I've found doors ajar when I know I've closed them. Once I would swear that one of the beds had been slept on. Not in, but that someone had laid down on it during the night."

"It couldn't have been Maxine or one of the other housekeepers taking a break? Or even the manager and you just didn't notice it sooner?"

"No, because . . ." And she looked away. "You're going to think I'm silly, but I check the place over at night before I go to bed."

Annie asked, "How many people have you given keys to?"

"No one."

"Not even Big Al?"

"Well, yes, he did have one, but why would he come sneaking back in and taking things that didn't belong to him while leaving things that did?"

"I don't know. Has anyone shown an interest in buying

the property? If that were the case, our culprit might be a thwarted buyer."

"If only that were the case. But no one has shown an interest since I've been here. Which, when you think about it, is surprising. The lodge itself is in excellent condition and the hot springs could easily be developed into a real draw."

Annie saw an opening and took it. "Then why haven't *you* done that, Trilby? If you were to advertise the hot springs, I'd be willing to bet you'd fill this place year-round."

"Because frankly it has seemed too overwhelming to even contemplate. You can't just do things willy-nilly because they seem like a good idea. It takes money and there are hoops of all kinds to jump through. I'm tired, Annie, and losing my job in Seattle and then Brad did nothing to enhance my self-confidence. Fully developing this place— on my own—has seemed beyond what I could tackle. At least at this time."

Annie could understand that it would be quite a project, but she also knew half measures rarely worked. Whispering Pines had so much potential that Trilby was ignoring. "You could have the locks changed at least."

"I know, and I did look into it. There's absolutely no one around here who does that sort of thing. And I can't afford to pay someone to come from a distance. Besides," and she shuddered, "changing the locks won't stop things happening outside."

"Like what?"

"Four times since I've been here I've discovered fresh flowers on that memorial grave in the woods."

That did give Annie a chill. "You're not serious?"

"Very."

"Can you attach any significance to the times you found flowers there?"

"What do you mean?"

"Were the dates significant? Perhaps there's someone

around who knew Wilbur Watkins and wants to keep his memory alive—at least within themselves. An old friend—or even an old love."

Trilby's look of relief was transforming. "That's a reasonable explanation. Why didn't I think of it? That's probably exactly the case. And the dates the flowers appear undoubtedly have some significance for the person leaving them." She managed a sincere little laugh. "Here I've been attaching some sinister meaning to them. Oh, Annie, I can't thank you enough. You've cleared up at least one little mystery. I knew you'd be able to help me."

Trilby visibly relaxed and Annie hoped that would translate into more enthusiasm for upcoming events. She herself wanted to be able to concentrate on the workshops and not have to worry about what was going on behind the scenes. Perhaps now the rest of the week would roll along without a hitch. No sooner had she tempted the fates with that thought than a piercing scream echoed through the lodge.

They hurried as quickly as possible to the source of the scream and found Maxine there seconds before them trying to calm a somewhat distraught Louella Haven.

Annie found her voice before Trilby. "What's wrong?" She was surprised that the two words came out on a gasp, which suggested more anxiety than she would have been comfortable admitting. It would seem Trilby's anxiety was contagious.

Louella's eyes behind her glasses were huge. "A rat! I came into the room and surprised a rat! It was huge! Monstrous! It chased me. If I hadn't jumped up on that chair it would have gotten me."

Maxine slapped her thighs and burst into laughter. "If that rat had wanted to get you, lady, it wouldn't have been stopped by anything so close to the ground as that there chair. It would have run right up the chair leg and onto yours. Might even have come up and sat on your shoulder. I'll bet it was as scared of you as you were of it. More so probably when it heard you scream. You about gave *me* heart failure."

Trilby couldn't share in Maxine's mirth. "Are you positive it was a rat?"

Louella drew herself up to her full four foot eight inches. "Young woman, I know a rat when I see one. It was definitely a rat!"

It was Maxine who more or less saved the day. "What kind of a tail did it have?"

Louella hesitated, and Maxine answered for her with another question. "Did it have a bushy tail?"

"Rats don't have bushy tails."

"Well, I'm askin' you if this one did. Because I'm bettin' what you saw was a pack rat."

Louella seemed to settle down a bit. "Are they dangerous?"

"Why, they'll carry your socks off given half a chance and that's while they're still on your feet." And with that and a small smile only Annie noticed, Maxine returned to her cleaning.

Trilby tried to reassure Louella. "Really, I don't think you need to worry about pack rats or the regular kind. We do live in the woods and sometimes critters get in, but they don't mean any harm. And I'm sure they would never hurt anyone."

Louella gave a slight harumph. "Nevertheless, I'll be certain to keep all my valuables locked up in my suitcase."

Once the door closed behind her, Trilby turned to Annie. "What more can go wrong?"

"Trilby, it's like you yourself just said. We're in the woods and critters are bound to wander in once in a while."

"But rats, regardless of what kind they are, seem so—so seedy."

Had Trilby already forgotten the one they'd found that morning? "Then perhaps you should set some traps in out-of-the-way places where your guests won't find them but the rodents will."

"Good idea."

A few minutes later they parted company outside of An-

nie's room. Annie entered cautiously and shut the door behind her, then glanced around before walking over to the
bureau. She was no fonder than Louella of rats, regardless
of what kind of tail they had. Things seemed fine until she
glanced at the top of the bureau. Something was missing.

Chapter Nine

Annie studied the items on top of the bureau for a moment before it dawned on her what should have been there but wasn't. It was the necklace she'd found earlier by the old bathhouses. Of all the things for someone to take. The chain was knotted and broken, and the small gemstone, if indeed it was a real gem, was filthy. She could only guess how long it had been embedded in the dirt. Then she recalled Trilby mentioning earlier that one of the few guests she'd managed to attract had reported an earring missing. Perhaps Louella's rat really had been a pack rat. If so, was it responsible for some of the lost objects?

Annie plumbed the depths of her memory for anything she might know about pack rats, but all she could come up with was the idea they were attracted to bright, shiny objects. The necklace she'd found didn't exactly qualify, but perhaps Louella's rat had visited and, seeing something it liked, made off with it. There seemed no other plausible explanation, unless Maxine had developed a liking for tarnished, dirt-encrusted jewelry. Which Annie seriously doubted. Maxine might like to talk, but Annie would bet she was as honest as the day was long. Was there any way of following up on her pack-rat theory?

While mulling it over in her mind, Annie wandered over

to the window in time to see Louella Haven heading off
into the woods that fringed the back of the property. Annie
had but a minute to take in the fact that she had discarded
her hat for a yellow bandanna scarf and her floral print
dress in favor of baggy pants. Evidently she'd had a quick
recovery from her rodent encounter and now felt equal to
meeting any wildlife she might run across. Annie felt uncomfortable with the thought of the older woman hiking
by herself and decided to follow at a discreet distance.

Annie slipped out a side door and hurried into the timber
before anyone could stop her. Disappointedly, Louella had
enough of a head start that she was nowhere to be seen,
and there was no clue as to where she might have gone
other than the direction Annie had seen her take minutes
ago. It was at least a starting point, and Annie decided to
take it. She hadn't gone far before she ran across a well-
trodden path leading to a glassy-surfaced lake. Annie
stopped, marveling at water so clear she could see the lake
bottom and silvery fish. The surface was unruffled by even
so much as a light breeze except where an occasional fish
jumped, creating a ripple effect. Trees reflected on the pristine surface as if it were a looking glass.

While at first glance the water looked absolutely still,
she saw that it really wasn't. Where it met the shore there
was the slightest movement. Kneeling down she swished
her hand in the water and discovered it was quite cold.

At some time, several trees had been cut down, but their
stumps remained. Annie sat down and took in the peacefulness of her surroundings. The scene was primeval and
she wouldn't have been at all surprised to see a High Cas-
cade version of the Loch Ness monster rise up from the
depths, a stem of greenery coyly dangling from its mouth.
While no such fantasy creature put in an appearance, a
black bear did ramble out of the timber on the other side
and head for the lake. She watched while it caught a fish
and then ambled back into the timber. She'd lost sight of
Louella and couldn't help worrying that the older woman

might encounter a bear of her own. Of all the things she worried about in conjunction with her workshops, it wasn't that someone might be attacked by some form of wildlife. Annie stood up and with a tinge of anxiety wondered which direction the woman had taken.

Annie knew her conscience wouldn't let her return to the lodge without trying to locate Louella. The High Cascades wilderness was free of the thick underbrush that characterized the coast and so she was able to walk along the lake without any trouble. Repeatedly she was impressed by the clearness of the water and the absolute peacefulness of her surroundings. She willed herself not to let anxiety spoil the mood-healing quality of nature's cathedral. She drew in several deep breaths while willing herself not to obsess over Louella Haven's whereabouts. No doubt she was an experienced hiker, and she certainly had more life experience than Annie. Just when Annie almost had herself convinced that there was no good reason to be concerned over Louella, a piercing, almost inhuman, scream shattered the tranquility of the late afternoon.

Annie stopped dead in her tracks, understanding for perhaps the first time what that tired old cliché really meant. The hair stood up on the back of her neck and fear knotted her stomach. It was the same unearthly cry she and Brendan had heard the night before. It had been terrifying then, and knowing it was probably a cougar made it no less so. Would Louella hear it and panic? Or had she perhaps met the creature head-on? Annie turned and hurried back the way she'd come, making no attempt to be quiet. If she made enough noise perhaps she might scare anything off that was in her vicinity. She couldn't tell from the scream whether the animal was nearby or if the sound just carried in the relative silence of the wilderness. More than once she tripped and almost fell, saving herself from a nasty fall by grabbing at a tree. Sooner than she had expected she broke into the clearing behind the lodge, only to discover Trilby, Maxine, and Louella in the yard.

It was Trilby who spoke first. "Annie, did you hear that? We wondered where you were. . . ."

Annie tried to catch her breath, but it took several seconds to do so. By then she'd decided not to mention that she'd been following Louella—or trying to, at least. "Yes, I heard it. It's a cougar, I think."

Maxine nodded in agreement. "I don't think there have been any this close by in a long time. In fact, I don't know of anybody who's claimed to have seen one in years. It's enough to raise the hair on the back of your neck though."

"Oh, surely it's not a cougar." Trilby didn't seem to want to believe they were right. She had enough to contend with without giant cats outside her back door. Annie marveled at Trilby's tendency to discount anything she didn't want to confront.

Maxine glanced at her employer. "Got any better ideas?"

Louella stood up from the stump she was perched on. "I think the girls are right and I would suggest, Annie, that you warn everyone attending the workshop not to stray very far from the lodge while they're here. At least not by themselves."

Trilby looked as if she could cry. "I don't want there to be a cougar around here. I will never get any guests if they're afraid they'll be eaten alive."

After Trilby turned and went inside, Louella glanced from Annie to Maxine. "What does she mean about getting guests? I'd have thought they'd be standing in line to stay here."

Maxine cracked her gum. "People can't seem to find anything to do."

Louella gave a hoot of disbelief. "With all this wilderness to explore? Why would anyone even come here if they didn't want to hike and fish?"

Maxine turned on her way back to the lodge. "Beats me."

Brendan was making himself a cup of coffee when Annie walked into the kitchen. "Was that our friend the cougar we heard?" he asked.

"I guess, and he didn't sound any great distance away—that's for certain. Louella thinks I should warn everyone not to stray far from the lodge."

"I think you should tell them there's a cougar in the vicinity, yes."

"But Brendan, the animal sounds so chilling when it screams. So fierce and predatory."

"It's a wild animal, Annie—and a lot more familiar with the back country than any of us. It might be a good idea if none of us ventured off on our own."

She thought of Brendan's solitary morning walks. "Does that mean you'll curtail your outings?"

He shrugged and gave her the grin she usually found so endearing, but this time maddening. "Ask me no questions and I'll tell you no lies."

"Brendan!"

"I'll be careful, Annie, promise. But how can I find the mysterious stone maiden if I stay indoors?"

"She's not that important . . ."

"I think you might be wrong there."

Much to Annie's surprise, Trilby stayed focused long enough to fix them a superb spaghetti dinner. Following that, Annie spent a couple of hours with last-minute preparations for the workshop ahead. Namely, setting up the room where the gathering would be held. People would be arriving tomorrow and she wanted everything in place. There were packets to be assembled containing style and market information, suggestions for overcoming writer's block, and places to look for ideas. Darkness had settled in long ago by the time she looked up from the table where she'd been working. It was past time for her to turn in for the night.

Annie switched off the lights, only to notice a pinpoint of light moving across the grounds. She resisted the temptation to turn the dining room lights back on and hurried instead to a side door that would allow her access to the outside. She opened the door cautiously, trying to make as little noise as possible, but hoping to identify who was out there without giving herself away. Just then the intruder stepped from the cover of the trees and Annie realized whoever it was was returning to the lodge, not passing by. She stepped back into the protection of the recessed doorway and hoped she could see without being seen. Annie almost betrayed herself by gasping in surprise when she recognized Louella. Now what in the world was the older woman doing out on her own—at night and with a cougar in the vicinity?

Annie awoke to another sunny but chilly morning. The sheets where she hadn't been laying were icy cold and her feet felt in need of a pair of socks. After braving the bare floor, she hurried into the bathroom and turned on the shower. Workshop attendees would be arriving throughout the day so she was determined on an early start.

As she hurried to the kitchen, spurred on by the unbeatable aroma of fresh perked coffee, she was surprised not to encounter anyone on her way. Where was Maxine and her best friend the vacuum?

She'd halfway expected to find Trilby busy in the kitchen, but the only person there was Brendan.

"Good morning, Sleepyhead," Brendan teased.

"Good morning to you too. What has you up so early?"

"Couldn't sleep, so I thought I might as well get up and get going. So far no one else seems to be stirring unless they're already up and out of here."

"It might be a little early for Maxine and the others are probably asleep. I know for a fact that Louella was up as late as I was last night."

"And how do you know that?"

Annie made herself some toast and poured a cup of coffee while explaining what she'd witnessed before turning in for the night. "I figured I would nonchalantly mention that I'd seen a light moving across the yard last night and see if she admits it was her."

"Can't hurt to try, but don't do it within Trilby's hearing. She's jumpy enough as it is. I have to admit it makes me curious what Louella was doing prowling around at that hour. Especially as she was so keen on warning people to stay close to the lodge. Where does our little friend go? But I guess we can't lock her in her room at night."

"She screamed bloody murder when she thought there was a rat in her room, so I'm a little surprised she's brave enough to venture into the woods at night where we know there are bears and cougars."

"Perhaps she wasn't really frightened of the rat but saw it as an opportunity to establish a false vulnerability." He grinned at Annie. "A red herring to you, Ms. Mystery Author."

"Somehow I don't associate red herrings with Louella Haven. Anyway, why would she want to do that? What would be the point?"

He shrugged. "I haven't gotten that far in my reasoning."

"You're no help, although I have a way you could be if you wanted. That is, when and if you're ready to take a break from your writing."

"And what would you like me to do?"

"Perhaps you could find out if there's a library anywhere near here, and if so, maybe you'd have the time to see if they have a copy of an old book Trilby told me about. It's the journal of a woman who explored this backwoods country on horseback some time in the 1930s."

"And why is this of interest to you?"

"This intrepid woman claims actually to have seen the rock carving we've been hearing about."

"Trilby knows about this book but doesn't have a copy?"

"She can't find it."

"That figures. No wonder that woman was downsized from her job. She's about as organized as the countryside after a hurricane has moved through."

"Brendan!"

"Come on, Annie, your friend is her own worst enemy."

"I know—I think it's just that she feels overwhelmed so much of the time, and just when she does get going she meets a setback and that stymies her."

"You know how I feel about Trilby, so there's no sense hashing it over again. Tell me, why do you want to locate this journal?"

"It might give us a clue to the location of this rock sculpture. Obviously it's still accessible because Trilby's erstwhile manager sketched it."

"That might not have been because he'd seen it. He might simply have been sketching what he thought it was like after hearing about it."

"Nevertheless, I'd like a look at that journal if possible."

"Okay—I'll see what I can do." Brendan knew he couldn't stop Annie from investigating anything once she put her mind to it. And he had to admit he was curious himself about this rock carving and the lore that seemed to have grown up around it. At the same time he hadn't forgotten his own resolve to find out where the elderly man from the Log Cabin Café was camping. And then there was the time he needed to invest in his own writing. He could see that the days weren't going to be long enough. A recurring problem since he'd met Annie.

They heard footsteps in the hallway and waited expectantly to see who was about to join them. Brendan had been hoping to have Annie all to himself for breakfast, but since that seemed impossible, he took this opportunity to excuse himself. Louella pulled off gloves and a jacket and draped them over a chair before going to pour herself some coffee. "It's chilly out there this morning, although I've had quite a walk."

Annie, despite her worries, smiled at Louella's enthusiasm. "I hope you left a trail of breadcrumbs so you wouldn't get lost."

"Oh, pooh! I couldn't get lost if I tried. Besides, I simply followed the trail to the lake and them walked around it. There was no chance of losing my way."

"You should know that I spotted a bear across the lake yesterday."

"Really, now I would like to have seen that." And Louella pulled a small camera from her jacket pocket. "I'm always on the lookout for a good snapshot. Pictures make a good story better."

Annie thought this a good opportunity to find out about Louella's writing experience. Her comment made Annie wonder if she had a journalism background.

"Tell me, Louella, have you done a lot of writing over the years?"

Did she imagine the sudden sparkle in the older woman's eyes? "Oh, I've done a piece here and there for our local paper. Mostly human interest. Nothing too gritty."

"Your letter mentioned that you were interested in writing a novel."

"My dear, by the time you've lived as long as I have you will have witnessed a number of things you can't explain. And you'll want to solve what really happened, even if you can't prove you're right."

"Am I correct in assuming that you intend to write about something that actually took place?"

The older woman sipped her coffee. "Doesn't every bit of fiction have a grain of truth in it?"

Before Annie could comment, Louella continued. "Have you ever wondered why some places seem to attract the unexplained? Like this place, for instance." Louella's bright twinkling eyes seemed to dare Annie to dispute her observation.

So Annie decided to see just how much Louella knew. "Meaning?"

"I've been reading up on the area. Old history books and diaries. I don't need to tell you they're a wealth of information. The hot springs suggest geothermal activity not far below the surface of the ground, and last night I saw a strange flashing light in the sky."

Annie was excited that Louella had seen the lights in the night sky, although she herself had missed last night's display. It also gave her the opening she'd been looking for. "Speaking of lights, I saw one moving across the property late last night, just before I went up to bed."

"Oh, really? Does that mean we can add prowlers to our list of the unexplained?"

"So far it's a short list." Annie was disappointed and more than a bit curious that Louella failed to own up to her own night-time foray. What exactly did that failure mean?

Chapter Ten

Trilby came rushing into the kitchen, distraught as usual. "Thank heavens I've found you. The day's hardly started and we already have a problem."

Annie wanted to caution her about saying anything like that in front of a guest, but it was too late. Fortunately, Louella was polite enough to gather up her coat and gloves and leave the room. "What is it, Trilby?"

Trilby sank down onto one of the kitchen chairs. "We've had someone arrive who isn't registered. And she's anything but happy that we didn't receive her registration. She acts like we've deliberately destroyed it."

Annie stifled a groan. She and Trilby had already discussed what to do in the event someone unexpected arrived. She could well imagine that her friend, rather than putting the woman at ease, had let her know how upset she was. "Trilby, I thought we'd covered this possibility. Did you explain there had been some trouble with the mail, but we were happy to have her and there was plenty of room for her?"

"No, I'm afraid I'd just had words with Maxine and so I was distracted."

"What's wrong with Maxine?"

"Oh, she picked today of all days to ask for a raise.

Claims she deserves one if she's going to be doing all the cleaning."

Annie had to admit that Maxine's timing was off. "You certainly can't argue with her logic. However, I think you need to get someone else here at least for the duration of the workshop. Especially now that there are seven people signed up."

"The employment agency in town won't send anyone. I told you that."

"Is there maybe a temp agency?"

"I don't know."

"Well, see if there is. And you may have to pay a little extra." She saw the stricken look on Trilby's face and wondered just how far in debt her friend might be. "Look, I'll waive any profit from the workshop. You can have my share if it will help things run smoothly. Okay? I don't want anyone to go away dissatisfied or unhappy if we can possibly help it."

"But it doesn't seem fair for you not to make any profit from this venture."

"Let's not worry about that now." Annie was more concerned about the reputation of the workshops she put on than any money she might make from them. "Now where is this unexpected guest?"

"She's seated in the lobby. I told her I'd have to consult with you as to whether or not we had a place for her."

Annie managed not to groan. "The important thing is, *do* you have a room for her?"

"I'm assuming the husband and wife coming will share a room, so yes, I do. If they each want their own room I don't know what we'll do." Trilby kept running her hands through her hair until she looked like she'd been attacked by large birds looking for nesting material.

"We'll simply tell them separate rooms aren't possible. Now I'll introduce myself to . . . did you get a name?"

Trilby looked more miserable than ever. "She told me,

but I promptly forgot. I was more concerned with what we were going to do with her."

"Well, I'm going to try and make her feel welcome. Why don't you get her room ready."

The woman in question was at first glance in her mid-forties. Her thick steel-gray hair was cut short in a style that accentuated her high cheekbones and large eyes. She was tall and obviously comfortable with herself, wearing jeans and a fisherman's knit sweater as if the style had been created just for her. A well-traveled suitcase, plastered with luggage labels that suggested she too was well-traveled, rested beside her on the floor. Annie had expected a powder keg waiting to explode, not this obviously laid-back woman who was probably rarely rattled by anything.

"Hello, I'm Annie Kirk." She sat down opposite the woman as if prepared for a chat.

The woman extended her hand. "And I'm Iris Barton, a great fan of yours. I was planning on attending your workshop, but that rather frazzled woman who greeted me seemed to be in doubt that it would be possible. I mailed in a registration, but apparently it went astray."

"You have to excuse Trilby, she's a bit overworked at the moment and I had told her the number attending the workshop was a firm six." Not exactly the truth, but a plausible explanation for Trilby's less-than-professional behavior. "But we're certainly not going to turn you away."

"That's a relief to hear."

"As long as we don't have more people show up than we have places for them to sleep, we're in good shape. So we'll just get you registered and then you'll be all set."

Trilby appeared at that moment, balancing a tray with two coffee mugs and a plate of cookies. "I thought you might like something after your long drive."

The woman sat up and smiled appreciatively. "Ahhh, I never say no to a good cup of coffee."

"I'll get a registration form and be right back." Annie hurried upstairs, rounded the corner to her room, and almost collided with Maxine, who had just parted company with Louella.

The housekeeper shifted conversational gears in an instant. "There you are." She glanced over her shoulder and, assuring herself that Louella was out of earshot, said, "I left some mail on your bureau."

Annie frowned and asked, "Today's mail?"

"No, some I found. You asked me to keep an eye out, remember?"

Annie nodded, recalling she had done exactly that. "Where did you find it?"

"Stuffed between some sheets in the linen closet."

"Thanks. I'll have a quick look right now."

"Well, don't be surprised at what you find."

"What do you mean?"

"You'll see." And she walked away.

There were three pieces of mail, two envelopes clearly marked ATTN: MYSTERY WRITING WORKSHOP. Annie slit them open and found not only Iris Barton's reservation, but Fran Shipman's. There was also a soiled envelope that had already been opened. Annie hesitated about half a second before reading it. It was another note calling Trilby a trespasser, along with a warning that all trespassers should be shot. It seemed likely that Trilby had been so upset by the hate mail she had stuffed it and the envelopes with it out of sight.

Annie took the reservations downstairs with her, deciding on the way what she would say to Iris Barton, who didn't seem to have a concern in the world other than sipping her coffee and nibbling a cookie. She smiled when Annie sat down opposite her. "It's a good thing you showed up. I was about to devour all of these cookies. Which means I'll have to take a brisk walk once I'm settled in. There are hiking trails around here, I assume."

"I don't know if they're hiking trails or game trails, but there are plenty of them. Just be careful, we've heard a cougar's cry and I spotted a bear yesterday on the other side of the lake."

"There's a lake nearby?"

Annie nodded and smiled at the memory of its glassy perfection. It was a perfect mirror of the world around it.

"Are there canoes or kayaks?"

Annie was pretty sure there weren't and realized here was another bet Trilby was missing. "I don't know, but I'll certainly find out."

"I would have brought mine if I'd known about the lake. There's no better way to relax than out on the water by yourself." The woman leaned forward while placing her empty coffee cup on the tray. "I have to confess that I'm not a novice writer. I am when it comes to mysteries, but I make a living as a travel and outdoor writer."

"That explains the labels on your luggage."

Iris glanced down and then back to Annie. "I have been around and I've seen a lot. I've climbed Kilimanjaro—made it all the way to the top. Cavorted with wild dolphins at Kaikoura, New Zealand, made the Tongariro Crossing in New Zealand despite a broken bone in my foot. Then there was the cave in Southeast Asia where spiders constantly rained down on our heads. I was the only one of our party to tough it out once the creatures reached the size of dinner plates. But then there isn't *anything* I won't do for a good story. Particularly an exclusive. I'm rather competitive."

Annie was aghast. "Spiders the size of dinner plates?"

"Oh, yes. They live in these caves and fall like rain from the ceiling. They aren't all that size, of course."

"It would only take one . . ."

Iris smiled. "Now I'd like to carry some of the things I've seen one step further and incorporate them into a piece of fiction. I've reached the point in my life where I'm ready to settle down in one place and put down roots—at least for awhile. To do that I need to be able to make a living. So I thought perhaps I could write a book. And since mysteries are my reading preference when I'm relaxing . . ."

"Then, by all means, we'll try to get you started. Now," and Annie laid Iris's reservation on the low table between them, "the lost has been found."

"My reservation!"

"Yes, yours and one other. It seems they were misplaced when they arrived and the housekeeper only just found them. So you're all set. I'll get Trilby to show you to your room."

Brendan drove away from the lodge with mixed feelings of relief and guilt since he knew he should be writing. Annie's interest in the near-mythical rock carving had piqued his. There was a story there, and perhaps once he'd finished the Coyle biography he could tackle a short article on the rock sculpture. That is, if they could find it. Last night he'd worked on his Coyle manuscript until he couldn't keep his eyes open, just so he could make a run to the local library today. He'd found an old phone book at the lodge and located the library's number. After calling, he discovered it was only twenty miles away from the town where he had shopped for groceries.

The golden aspen lining the highway gave way to red vine maple as he neared the town. A rushing river ran along one side of the town and gave it a picture-postcard look. He had no problem finding the library or a parking space right in front of the two-story brick building. Inside it smelled of books and the crisp fall air coming in through open windows. Leather chairs scattered about invited visitors to sit down and read. Several of them were occupied and gentle snores emanated from one as Brendan walked up to the librarian's desk.

A woman of indeterminate age and with glasses perched on top of her gray hair looked up from her work and smiled at him. "Can I help you?"

"I certainly hope so. I'm only visiting here for a short while—three weeks, actually—and I'm wondering if you might have an old book I've heard about. A journal written by a woman who explored the back country around here on horseback. I have no idea of the title or her name. I just know there's such a volume."

"I know the book you mean. Unfortunately it's in our reference collection and so can't be checked out. But you're welcome to look at it here."

"Can't ask for much more than that, unless you can shed some light on the rock carving of a Native American woman I've been hearing so much about."

"Oh, my goodness. Is that story still circulating? It never seems to go away for long even though there's scant proof she ever existed."

"You're sure of that?"

The librarian leaned her elbows on the counter and adjusted her half glasses on her nose. "Am I certain that she never existed? No. Do I know of any *proof* that she's out there somewhere in the wilderness, waiting to be rediscovered? Well-l-l, that's debatable. The author of the journal you want to look at does say she saw it. The author, Bertha Wing, even states she located an old Paiute woman who says the sculpture was ancient when she was young. This woman—I believe, an elder of her tribe—claimed the carving had been there since the beginning."

"Does the author of the journal give any clues as to location?"

"If she does they're either very general or very subtle. I never picked up on them, and as far as I know neither has anyone else. If someone had located it we'd have heard about it." She studied him for a moment. "Do you mind me asking how you came to know about it?"

"I'm staying at Whispering Pines Resort for three weeks and the subject came up."

"Oh, yes. I imagine it would since the disappearance years ago of two women looking for the illusive rock maiden was the death knell for the resort. Not that it wasn't in trouble before then, mind you, but that was, as they say, the straw that broke the camel's back. The women were staying at the resort and so it became guilty in their disappearance by simple means of association."

Brendan debated pursuing this conversation with the librarian to see if she would come up with anything new he could relate to Annie. The decision was taken out of his hands when she continued but on a different track. "The manager at the lodge was also interested in locating the sculpture. He's apparently an artist and wanted to sketch her. You might talk with him and see if he had any luck locating the original."

"I would, but he's no longer there and left no forwarding address when he left."

"How strange! When I chatted with him he seemed quite content with his job and settled in. But you never know about people, do you. Here one minute and gone the next. One moment and I'll get that book for you."

She was back within minutes. Brendan took the well-worn volume and found himself a vacant leather chair near a window. He leafed through the diary and saw there was a scattering of drawings. One by one he glanced at them, all the while with mentally crossed fingers that the author, Bertha Wing, had sketched the rock maiden. He was rewarded for his diligence three-quarters of the way through the volume. The sketch took up a whole page and was done in great detail. Brendan studied it for some time in the hopes of discovering some clue to its possible location, but he wasn't familiar enough with the area to zero in on anything. He wondered if the librarian would let him make a photocopy of the page.

He looked around to see if there was a copy machine, but the only one he could see was behind the librarian's counter. There seemed to be nothing he could do other than ask. She looked up from her work when he approached the desk. "Did you find anything helpful?"

"Just this drawing the author made. I was wondering if you'd photocopy it for me."

She studied him for a moment and then reached for the

book. "This is highly irregular." Nevertheless, she went over to the photocopier and carefully laid the book face down. Again, without saying a word, she handed him the copy, but kept the book. Brendan hadn't had a chance to read what Wing had written, but guessed no further access to the volume was the price of the photocopy. "Thanks!"

He'd turned away when she spoke to him again. "If you find the carving—I'd like to know about it."

"Certainly." And he left the library. As he drove back to the resort he wondered how this sketch compared with the one done by Trilby's manager. Would he find the one was simply a copy of the other?

Annie was sitting out on the porch when Brendan drove up. Was she just taking a break or was she waiting for him? She smiled as he climbed the steps to the lodge. "Where have you been?"

He sat down next to her. "The nearest library. What do you think of this?" And he handed her the photocopy. "It's from the journal of Bertha Wing, intrepid traveler." Then he told her about his experience at the library. "Let's see how it compares with Big Al's rendering."

They went into the lobby and retrieved Big Al's drawing pad from beneath the front counter. Then laid the two pictures side by side. Annie leaned against Brendan. "Are they a match?"

"Yes—no, look!" And he made no effort to keep the excitement from his voice. "Big Al shows a rock slide here to the side that's missing from Bertha Wing's."

The manager's drawing was three times the size of the photocopy and so details were much easier to make out in his, but Annie noticed something dark to the side of Wing's sketch. "What's that?"

Brendan leaned down for a closer look. "Maybe a cave entrance?"

"Right about where Big Al has drawn in a rock slide." Annie felt a surge of excitement, in spite of the odds against them or anyone finding the rock sculpture from an artist's sketch. "Brendan—do you think we could locate the carving from the other features in the area? The mountains, maybe?"

"I should have read what Bertha Wing had written before I asked the librarian for a photocopy. I might have learned something useful. Obviously—or so it would seem—Trilby's ex-manager located it, probably helped along by his artist's eye for detail. Now whether he stumbled across it on his own or from some clue in her journal we can only guess. I wonder if there are any maps available that date from the time Bertha Wing passed through. They just might list known caves."

"What about trying the Forest Service or the local historical society if there is one?"

"First thing tomorrow."

"Oh, Brendan! I can't help but feel excited that *we* might possibly solve a mystery that has remained unsolved for half a century."

He didn't want to remind her that there was a lot of unexplored wilderness out there, and that people better equipped than the two of them had tried with no luck. He'd seen Annie succeed before where others had failed and she just might do it again. For now, he had some writing to do.

By nine o'clock in the evening all the workshop participants had arrived and were happily settled in their rooms or getting to know one another. Trilby had come up with assorted sandwiches, a veggie tray, and a plate of cookies. There were insulated carafes with coffee and hot water for tea and more cookies left out on the counter of the registration desk, just in case anyone wanted a late-night snack.

Annie stretched and yawned. "I'm going to hit the hay. Tomorrow will be a full day and I want to get a good night's sleep."

Brendan nodded. "Good idea. I've got a few more pages

I want to rough out, which should free me up for some detective work tomorrow."

Annie sighed. "You don't know how much I wish I could go with you. You have to promise to tell me immediately if you find anything."

"I will."

Annie climbed the stairs for what she was sure was the millionth time that day. The only room she passed where she could hear any sounds was the one shared by the married couple, Carmen and Frank Potts. Otherwise all was quiet until she got to Louella Havens's door. She could hear the sound of footsteps, as if Louella was walking back and forth, back and forth. It also seemed that she was talking to herself, for Annie could hear her repeating, "What to do? What to do?"

Had something disturbed the older woman? It was impossible to find out without admitting she'd been eavesdropping. She'd just have to hope Louella would come to her if there was a problem. So, determined to mind her own business, Annie retired to her own room and her very comfortable bed. But sleep refused to do more than hover on the edges of her consciousness. She tried laying on first one side and then another, but nothing seemed to work and she watched the minutes slip by on her travel clock. Finally she could stand it no longer and got up to walk over to the window, pushing it wide and leaning out. Which turned out to be a mistake because the chilly mountain air jolted her completely awake.

What was her problem? Surely not nervousness over the upcoming workshop? She'd done the same thing dozens of times and thoroughly enjoyed them. So why couldn't she sleep? The night sky was spangled as usual with a dusting of stars that twinkled and planets that didn't. And of course there were the usual moving objects—probably nothing more exotic than planes and satellites, but who knew. Just as she had decided to go downstairs to the kitchen and fix herself a cup of warm milk, a flash of light briefly arced above the trees. It startled her and she stepped back, then braced herself against the wall when everything began to shake.

Chapter Eleven

The small quake lasted only seconds and she heard one or two squeals before her door burst open and she was in Brendan's arms. "Annie, are you okay?"

"I am. . . . That was so unexpected." She rested her head on Brendan's chest a little longer than was necessary. After all, she hadn't been frightened by the brief, sharp earthquake, only surprised. But being in Brendan's arms was far too pleasant an experience to end prematurely. Within a matter of minutes, the room seemed to be full of people all asking questions at once and their brief period of intimacy was over.

"What was that?"

"Are we in any danger?"

"Will there be another?"

It was impossible to sort out who was saying what, and to Annie's surprise it was a sleepy-sounding Trilby who took charge of the explanations. "It was a little quake—nothing to worry about. We often have them because this is still a geologically active area. I'm told little quakes are good because the earth is stretching, and when you have little ones pressure is being relieved. So it's nothing to be concerned about. Truly."

Annie wondered if Trilby knew what she was talking

119

about but wasn't about to question her. She didn't want anyone jumping ship because the earth shook a bit. She'd taken inventory of who was present while Trilby talked and noticed that Louella was the only one absent. Did that mean the oldest member of their group had slept through the slight tremor or that she was perhaps wandering about again? Annie couldn't imagine that Louella would have slept through both the slight quake and the commotion that followed. Louella seemed the least likely person to be an enigma, yet that's what she was turning out to be.

Once everyone returned to their rooms, Annie shared her suspicions with Brendan, who answered, "Why don't you simply check her room? It would be perfectly natural to make sure she's all right. In fact, thoughtful."

"You're right." But Louella wasn't in her room or anywhere else they looked. Annie couldn't help but be a little worried. "Should we go looking for her?"

"No, we should not." Brendan was emphatic on that point. "If she's foolish enough to go prowling around out there in the dark then she can find her own way back or wait until daylight to be found. If we really knew our way around in this area then it would be one thing. But we don't, and neither one of us needs to get lost—or worse. She knows the dangers of the area."

"But where do you suppose she goes?"

"Maybe she suffers from insomnia. And she may not go far at all. If she isn't back by daylight, I'll go looking for her. Now you really should try to get some sleep."

Annie knew he was right, but it didn't put her mind at ease. Then she noticed that Brendan didn't return to his room, but headed downstairs. She hurried to her window and saw a flashlight move across the yard. He was having a look around. Annie didn't know whether to be worried or relieved. She climbed into bed, resolved to listen for his return, but instead fell asleep.

* * *

The heavenly smell of coffee woke her and she opened her eyes to see Maxine standing at the foot of her bed with a breakfast tray. "Mornin'. How'd you like last night's excitement?"

"It was certainly entertaining." She scooted up against the headboard. "Does Trilby have you doing double duty? You shouldn't be waiting on me."

"I don't know where Miz Watkins is this morning. Mr. Marshall's the one who asked me if I would help with breakfast and bring you up a tray. And I must say it's a pleasant change from vacuuming and making beds. I don't know where Miz Watkins goes at night, but every morning there's dirt on the hall carpets."

"Every morning—or just the last couple of days?" Perhaps Maxine was blaming Trilby when she should be accusing Louella.

"Every morning since I've been comin' to work here. She jumps at shadows, but she must be goin' somewhere at night."

Annie said nothing, but she recalled that Trilby had claimed someone was getting in at night no matter how secure she made the lodge. Was that someone to blame for the tracks on the carpets? "Thanks for the coffee, Maxine. I certainly needed a wake-up call this morning. Trilby told everyone last night that there are often small quakes around here. Is she right, or was she just trying to put everyone's mind at ease?"

"Probably some of both. We do get little earth twitches now and again, but not generally as much shakin' as last night."

"You don't think it's anything to worry about?" Annie asked.

"No—it's just a little atmosphere for all your would-be writers."

"Then I guess I should thank Mother Nature."

"I guess maybe you should. She could have given us a lot harder shake."

"You say you don't know where Trilby is this morning?"

"Haven't seen her." Maxine shrugged.

"What about Louella Haven?"

"Chowin' down in the kitchen when I left."

Annie's sense of relief was immense. She was bothered by the notion that Trilby was nowhere to be found, but she didn't have the time now to follow up on her friend's probable whereabouts. She had to get up and around. Annie liked being comfortable at all times and especially when conducting one of her workshops. So she chose a pair of gray flannel slacks and a bright yellow sweater that complemented her auburn hair. Then fastened a pair of gold earrings in her ears.

She could hear activity in the rooms she passed, but was the first to arrive in the room set aside for the workshop. Someone had arranged an appealing assortment of breakfast rolls, breads, and scones. And of course there was both coffee and tea. Annie helped herself to more coffee and a muffin. The small room was the perfect size—not too big and not too small. They could feel cozy but not cramped. Mullioned windows looked out on a small grove of aspen and ground covered with a carpet of gold. Sunlight filtering through the trees cast leafy shadows inside the room. Annie thought the very atmosphere inspiring and hoped everyone else felt the same. She promised a lot in her workshops, and the right ambiance certainly helped her deliver on those promises.

People wandered in and Annie let her gaze roam the room. Everyone was accounted for but Louella Haven. Maxine had said she was eating earlier. So where was she now that they were only five minutes away from the starting time?

Annie listened to the friendly chatter going on around her and tried not to worry, but the next time Maxine appeared to refresh the breakfast tray she excused herself for a moment and went over to speak with the housekeeper.

"Maxine, I'm a little concerned about Louella. I know

you said you'd seen her earlier, but we're about ready to
get started and she hasn't put in an appearance. Could you
maybe help me out by going up to her room and seeing if
she's there? I know we're asking a lot of you, but as you
know, we're shorthanded."

"No problem. I'll be glad to check. Probably she's just
not back from her morning walk. We'll just have to hope
she hasn't disappeared or been breakfast for that cougar we
keep hearin'."

"Maxine, you're awful."

"Ain't it a fact."

Annie held off starting the workshop partly because
everyone was having such a good visit and she felt camaraderie between participants was important, but also because Louella still hadn't shown up and Maxine hadn't
returned. But they were fifteen minutes into the first hour
and she couldn't postpone getting started much longer. She
glanced toward the door one more time and saw Maxine
shrug and shake her head. So Louella was whereabouts
unknown at the moment.

It was Iris Barton who made up her mind for her. "I
know you're waiting on that older woman, but I for one
am eager to get started."

"We will." Annie stood up then and went to the front of
the room where she'd set up a podium and a table covered
in books and handouts. "I want to welcome everyone once
again. I'm sorry we're a little late, but one of our members
hasn't shown up yet and I was waiting for her. However,
I think we'd best get started. I'm Annie Kirk—and I see
you've been getting to know one another. Nevertheless,
let's go around the room and introduce ourselves. You
might want to tell us why you're here. Fran, let's start with
you."

The woman elected to start pushed her chair away and
stood up. "Hi, I'm Fran Shipman. I'm from Portland and I
love to read mysteries. I've worked as an RN for the last

twenty-five years and I'm ready to try something different. Maybe try my hand at creating a crime-solving nurse."

Carmen and Frank Potts stood up together. She was a flamboyant redhead who evidently thought the more makeup the better. He was a gray little man who had the look of someone who never smiles, but he was the one who did the talking. "We're Carmen and Frank and we've been writing romances under the name Daphne Moore. We've made a good living, but after fifteen years of unbridled passion we're ready to try something new and thought mysteries might be the next logical step."

"Hi, I'm Jackie Marks and I'm here all the way from Seattle. During the day I work behind a cosmetics counter, but at night I write and write and write." Jackie was a breathy little blond with wispy hair and impossibly blue eyes. *Contacts,* Annie decided. *She wears colored contacts.* "I love Annie's books and I want to be just like her."

Oh, dear, Annie thought. *Why does there have to be one case of hero worship in each group?*

Jocelyn Curtiss, a slightly round brunette, had come the shortest distance since she lived in the city of Bend. "I have to confess I'm a workshop junkie. When I read about this one I knew I had to attend. I don't know if I can learn to write a mystery or not, but I can sure try. I've tried my hand at every other genre." Laughter greeted her remarks.

Iris Barton rose gracefully from her chair. "I guess that leaves me. My name is Iris Barton and I'm a travel writer. But I've reached the stage where I'm ready to put down roots, and since I'm never without a mystery to read I thought I could perhaps try writing one. I've certainly been enough places to give one an exotic flair."

Annie smiled. She'd developed a sixth sense for the people who attended her workshops and she could tell this was a good mix. "Thanks. Well, that leaves only our absent member, Louella Haven. We'll have to hope she doesn't miss too much of the morning. Okay, you're here to learn to write mysteries. So let's get started. Inside each of your

packets you'll find a sealed envelope. The one that says
Don't open until instructed. Inside each envelope you'll
find a card inscribed with a murder weapon. I want you to
write a murder scene using the weapon on your card. No
groaning, no comparing notes. Stretch yourselves out of the
familiar territory we all inhabit as writers. You'll have
thirty minutes to write the scene that is the backbone of
your story. Then we'll talk about them, and those of you
who want can read what you've written to the rest of us."
Annie went around the room, smiling encouragement in the
face of dismayed looks when people saw what their envelopes contained. "Remember now, you have half an hour."

Once they'd all begun writing, she hurried to the kitchen.
Brendan was sitting at his laptop writing furiously and
drinking coffee. "Have you seen either Trilby or Louella?"

He shook his head. "No, I haven't."

"I wonder where they are?"

"With Louella, who knows. With Trilby, I could make
an educated guess. Why aren't you with your group?"

"They're doing a writing assignment at the moment. So
I'm checking up on the missing. I have to admit I'm a bit
concerned about Louella since she likes to wander off."

"I'm sure she'll turn up."

Annie returned to the seminar room and with one eye on
the clock watched everyone writing with purpose. No one
appeared to be suffering from writer's block. They were all
so intent that she gave them an extra five minutes.

"Okay, times up. Would anyone like to read what
they've written?" She certainly hoped so, since sometimes
she had to prod people to get them to read aloud.

Jackie Marks hesitantly held up her hand. "I would—I
think."

Jackie stood up, swallowed and began reading in a shaky
voice that grew more confident as she became caught up
in her story. " 'Della James, comfortably propped up in bed
and absorbed in her vintage mystery novel complete with
lurid cover, felt safe despite the fact she was recuperating

from a car accident in which she'd suffered many broken bones. She couldn't get around without the aid of a walker and even then only short distances. But she was alive and mending with nothing to do but read. Her husband had left her alone for about an hour while he attended a night meeting. Della was enjoying the solitude when all the lights went out. She held her breath and tried not to panic. Power outages weren't unusual in the winter. Her husband would return soon and light some candles. Even though she tried to remain calm, the minutes crawled by and she strained to identify every sound. When she heard the door from the basement garage open, relief surged through her. "Frank— that is you, isn't it?" There was no response. "Frank! Frank?" A board creaked and Della struggled painfully to get out of bed, but without success. A firm hand pushed her backwards and a suffocating softness pressed across her face soon ended all her worries.' "

Jackie sat down to a smattering of applause.

"Jackie, that's a wonderful scene. It raises a lot of questions and opens the door to a lot of possibilities for development. And your murder weapon was. . . ." Annie knew the answer was obvious, but she wanted to make certain Jackie hadn't substituted one of her own choosing.

"A pillow."

"Well, you made good use of it. Anyone else care to share?"

It seemed everyone did and the next forty-five minutes sped by. "Okay, you're all off to a good start. Now I want you to describe your victim and develop at least three reasons why someone might want to kill him or her."

The session moved along, but lunch came and went without sight of Louella. They were about to break for the day when Jocelyn Curtiss raised her hand.

"Yes, Jocelyn?"

"What do you know about the two women who disappeared years ago while staying here? Is it the reason you chose Whispering Pines for your workshop?"

Annie walked across to stand in front of the windows. "While their disappearance contributes a sense of mystery, I hadn't heard about it until after I arrived. Does everyone else know what Jocelyn is talking about?"

Jackie Marks raised her hand. "I don't."

Fran Shipman shook her head. "Neither do I."

Briefly, Annie related the story as she knew it.

When Annie finished, Jocelyn nodded, but added. "My understanding is that the two women worked for a Portland newspaper and they'd been sent to do an exposé on the resort. It was their paper that raised a ruckus over their disappearance. And their paper also kept it alive when it showed signs of becoming a nine-day-wonder. The suggestion was always there that they'd disappeared because they intended to expose false claims the owner of the resort was making for the hot springs and the people who had been cured by them."

This was news to Annie. "I hadn't heard that part of the story, but it explains why their disappearance took on the momentum it did."

Fran interjected. "Perhaps we could speculate on what might have happened to the women. It's certainly a mystery."

Annie was willing to bounce ideas around. "How about we get together after dinner. We'll consider it sort of an extra credit assignment. Anyone who wants to can come back here at, say, seven o'clock. It's not mandatory, but it might be fun to exchange theories."

Frank Potts removed his glasses and rubbed eyes that always looked red and tired. "Why should we think we can succeed where others failed?"

"Perhaps we can't. But it's an intriguing puzzle and would be a good exercise in problem solving. Which is at the heart of every successful mystery."

Several heads nodded, but Annie doubted she'd see the Pottses at the evening session. She was surprised however when they gathered together after the residue of dinner was cleared away. Candles glowed and there were carafes of coffee and hot water as well as a selection of desserts.

Annie was the first to arrive, followed closely by Louella Haven. "Louella, I'm glad you decided to join us. We missed you today."

Louella looked away. "I got lost this morning—couldn't find my way back to the lodge until early afternoon. I was completely exhausted so I took a nap."

Annie was instantly concerned. "Are you okay?"

"Disappointed I missed the workshop."

"Maybe we can go over some of the main points one-on-one before you have to leave."

"You'd do that for me?"

"Sure, why not?"

They were soon joined by Jocelyn Curtiss, Jackie Marks, and, surprisingly, Carmen Potts. Carmen smiled and apologized for her husband's absence. "Frank's tired, and if I can be honest the switch from romance writing to mysteries is my idea—not his. He feels we should stick with what we know we can write and sell. It is, after all, our bread and butter. I'm the one who's bored with heavy breathing and colorful innuendoes."

Annie couldn't hold back a chuckle. "I can understand his thinking, but there's no reason why you can't write in both genres."

"That's what I keep telling him." Carmen's flamboyant red hair and glamour-shot makeup were misleading. She wasn't at all confident or particularly outgoing. When she was being candid, she admitted they were part of her romance-writer look. Annie watched while she poured herself a cup of coffee, then laced it with cream and three heaping teaspoons of sugar, then piled a napkin with several cookies.

Annie waited a few more minutes to see if Iris Barton or Fran Shipman would decide to join them. By 7:20 she decided it was just going to be the five of them. A number nicely accommodated at one of the round tables. Annie was seated so she had both a view of the door and the windows which now looked out on darkness. There were no yard lights to illuminate the outside and no draperies to cover the windows. They could be seen while not seeing.

Jocelyn Curtiss brought along a bulging file folder of clippings relating to the disappearance of the two women. She actually blushed while explaining. "Living nearby I've heard the story so often that I've collected everything on it I could find. I didn't know how you'd be running the workshops or what we'd be expected to do. That's why I brought all this stuff with me."

Annie was impressed with Jocelyn's dedicated research. "No reason why you couldn't do something along that line."

"Can I take a look at the folder?" Annie passed it to Jackie. She could always look at it later, but frankly she'd heard so much about this event from so many different sources that she didn't feel she needed to read the clippings in order to discuss the subject. And Jackie was so interested. She was touched by the young woman's eagerness to learn everything presented. She was eighteen, just out of high school, and now on her own. She'd confided at dinner that she shared an apartment with three other girls, two of whom were flight attendants and not around very often. Her three roommates had come up with the workshop fee as her birthday gift. "They know how badly I want to be a writer. And how much I love your books." Jackie had arrived in a battered old Volvo that Annie hoped would make it back to Seattle. The young woman had talent, and Annie had resolved to offer her one of the scholarships available for a writing week at Harbor House.

When the others had had a chance to glance through the clippings, Annie asked, "Any theories as to what might have happened to these two women?"

Carmen was the first to volunteer. "Could they have arranged their own disappearance and then surfaced with new identities when everything had cooled down?"

"They were newspaper women sent here to get a story. I think they got more than they bargained for." Louella was very definite about this.

Jackie chimed in. "Were they really here to do an exposé of the resort?"

Jocelyn nodded. "Elmira Watkins had made extravagant claims for the hot springs on her property. The women had been sent to take a look at what was really going on here."

Annie deliberately said nothing, preferring to let the others take the lead. She was interested to see what they'd come up with.

Carmen polished off the last of her cookies and glanced longingly at the still full plate. "Maybe someone did them in. I mean, if they were going to do a tell-all piece on the resort."

Jocelyn nodded her agreement. "That possibility was considered, but eventually it was decided that there was no evidence of foul play. There was no evidence of anything really."

Jackie shivered with delight. "I think there's something so—so intriguing about the words *vanished without a trace*."

Annie nodded. "I agree that *vanished without a trace* opens up a wealth of possibilities. We just have to decide which of these is the most probable. I'd like to think that there is actually a trace—and that it's simply been over-looked."

Jackie rested her chin on her hands. "It would be so great if we could find them. Maybe their disappearance has something to do with those strange lights at night."

Carmen frowned. "Strange lights? I haven't seen any strange lights. What are you talking about?"

Annie explained what she had seen.

Jackie couldn't contain herself. "Maybe they're UFOs!"

Jocelyn Curtiss let out a hoot of laughter which dissolved into a fit of giggles. Finally she managed to gain control of herself enough to explain what she found so amusing.

"I'm sorry, I'm not laughing at you, Jackie. I suspect what you're seeing is earth lights. There's a lot of geothermal and minor earthquake activity in this area. People sometimes report seeing strange lights—some flashing, some like the Northern Lights—before quakes. While they're not particularly common in this area, they're also not an impossibility. Most of them are so minor that the average person misses them. I suspect they're so visible here because we're far from any town with neon lights, street lights, and other distractions. Theories as to what causes them vary, but there's nothing alien about them. Fascinating maybe, but certainly not from another world." She glanced around at disappointed faces. "Did I spoil a good story? I'm sorry, but knowing what they are doesn't make them any less mysterious."

They broke up shortly after that, leaving Annie to wonder if you could know the truth about something and still retain the mystery. She knocked on Brendan's door even though it was getting late. When he was slow answering the door she asked, "Did I wake you?"

"No—I was just finishing a sentence. What's up?"

"I thought you might be interested in an explanation Jocelyn had for the lights some of us have seen at night." She emphasized the *some of us*.

He gave her a dubious look. "Okay. . . ."

"It seems that the lights are known as earth lights and that they can be linked to geologic activity—like earthquakes. The kind that the ordinary person rarely notices. I don't think they know what causes the lights, but it does make a kind of weird sense. We know the Cascades aren't all dormant. Satellite photos have recently shown that the South Sister has a bulge uplift. As I understand it that means that magma or underground lava is slowly flowing into the area. Scientists are monitoring the event. There are hot springs aplenty, attesting to geothermal activity. Really, this is a very interesting place geologically. I find the whole thing fascinating."

"Does Jocelyn's explanation for the lights satisfy you?" Brendan asked.

"It does, but it's also made me wonder about a possibility . . ."

"And you couldn't wait to share this possibility with me."

She treated him to a mischievous grin he found very appealing. "That's right. Brendan, what if those two missing women were trapped in a landslide caused by an earthquake? We know the drawing by Trilby's missing manager differs from Bertha Wing's in that she shows an opening in the rock and he shows a tumble of rocks. They could have been exploring one of the many caves or lava tubes in the back country when a quake hit and been trapped."

"Leaving no evidence of where they'd been." Brendan could see the possibilities.

"Exactly. And if no one knew where they were, then no one would know where to start looking. When this workshop is over I'm going to do a little investigating into the earthquake history of this area."

"You're convinced you can find those women where others have failed, aren't you?"

"I guess maybe I am. But haven't I done just that before?"

"Yes, Annie, you have. But you might remember the price you almost paid for those solutions."

"Brendan, you worry too much."

"And you have too much of a tendency to think you're invincible."

Chapter Twelve

The nights were getting colder and the mornings were downright chilly. The lodge's heating system seemed to be inadequate and so Annie took it upon herself to build a fire in the fireplace of the lobby. It would at least give the illusion of warmth.

Louella was again absent from the morning session. When the two-hour lunch break rolled around, Annie passed Maxine in the hall and stopped her for a quick word. "Have you seen Louella?"

"Is she AWOL again?"

Annie nodded. " 'Fraid so."

"Want me to see if she's in her room?"

"Would you please?"

Maxine was back within minutes. "No Louella, but her stuff is still there. So she hasn't flown the coop."

"Thanks, Maxine. You're a gem."

"You better believe it—the best cubic zirconium. No doubt about it."

"Don't sell yourself short, girl."

Trilby was standing in the open doorway of the kitchen back door when Annie ran her to ground. She tapped Trilby on the shoulder. "You've outdone yourself today. Lunch looks delicious."

Trilby turned with a smile, although the troubled look wasn't completely gone from her eyes. "Surprised you, didn't I? But I think I'm getting into the swing of things."

"That's good. Speaking of someone who doesn't seem to have gotten into the swing of things, have you by any chance seen Louella?"

"No—has she gone missing again?"

"She's my worst nightmare at the moment. After going to great lengths to brag about her sense of direction, she claims to have gotten lost yesterday. Today I don't know whether to be annoyed or alarmed. Maxine checked and her suitcase is still in residence. Louella seemed contrite enough yesterday and I thought she'd learned a lesson, but apparently not. So where is she?" Maybe she was being overly suspicious, but Annie was beginning to wonder if Louella was attending the workshop only as a way to gain legitimate access to the property. Unbidden, the threats against Trilby surfaced.

Annie debated the wisdom of searching for Louella. Was there even the remotest possibility of finding her in the short span of time between workshop sessions? She knew she shouldn't go searching on her own. Brendan had already left for town and Trilby certainly wouldn't be her search-and-rescue partner of choice. Was there the possibility she could enlist Maxine's help?

Annie went looking for the housekeeper and found her taking a coffee break out in back of the lodge. "Maxine. . . ."

"Break over?"

"Only if you want it to be. Maxine, I'm concerned about Louella's absence. There's something not quite right about it—not two days in a row."

"I've been thinkin' the same thing. There's something a little bit furtive about her."

"I've got some time between the morning and afternoon sessions and I was wondering if you'd help me look for her."

"You think something might have happened to her?"

"I don't know, but I'd like to find out. It's a bit difficult for me to concentrate on the workshop when I'm wondering if she's okay or not."

Maxine stood up and dusted off the seat of her pants. "I guess I could do with a little exercise. Any idea which direction she might have gone?"

Annie drew in a deep breath and considered the question. "I spotted Louella prowling around the property late one night, although she didn't see me. I mentioned the next day that I'd seen a light moving around the grounds after dark because I wanted to see if she'd admit it was her. She didn't, and so . . ."

"You've begun to wonder why she's really here."

"Exactly. At her present rate of attendance she isn't getting her money's worth. Anyway, both times I've spotted the light it's been coming from the eastern edge of the property."

"Then let's have a look in that direction."

"Are you at all familiar with the wilderness behind the lodge?"

"When my old man was still alive we used to go huntin' in those hills. I suppose I can find my way around well enough that we won't get lost. Although I won't make any promises."

"Then you lead the way."

"Where angels fear to tread, huh?"

They'd walked along in silence for about five minutes when Maxine spoke. "You need to know that locals have pretty much avoided this area around here."

"Because of the things that are supposed to have happened at the lodge?"

"Because there's a lot of weird places—places even the animals won't go."

"Maxine, are you trying to scare this flatlander?"

"No, I like you and I wouldn't do that. I just want you to be prepared for anything."

Annie hurried to close the small distance between them. "Like what?"

"Hunters, hikers tell stories of getting into an area where their sense of direction gets all confused. Places where no birds sing and where no animals go, where it's easy to get lost because nothing is as it should be."

"You think Louella might have ventured into such a spot?"

"It's possible. It's also possible that we might."

"You don't think people could be exaggerating the existence of such areas?"

"I can't speak for others, but I can tell you my old man and I wandered into a mighty peculiar place once. We had our old hound dog with us and we noticed that instead of runnin' on ahead as she always did, she was laggin' behind. Then she just sat down and started howlin' fit to stand the hair up on the back of your neck. There'd been an early snowfall. Not much, just a skiff, but enough to spot animal tracks. That was when we noticed we were standin' in a circular area where there wasn't a track. Except for the ones we'd made. That old hound dog absolutely refused to enter that circle. And I have to tell you it wasn't many more seconds before I felt this peculiar feelin' that sent me scamperin' for high ground."

"What about your husband? Did he notice it also?"

"He laughed at me, but he darn near stepped on my heels followin' me to higher ground."

"What do you suppose caused the reaction you all had?"

"I don't know. I know old-timers talk of such places. They also claim the Native Americans knew about them and thought they were sacred. I think they're just plain scary. I know after my old man was gone my oldest boy and I tried to find the place again, but we never could."

"Let's hope you and I don't stumble across it today."

"Just so you know there's things out there we can't explain. . . ."

A chilling scream cut through the afternoon stillness. "I don't think I'd ever get used to hearing that."

"Does rattle your old bones, doesn't it?"

"Should we try to be quiet?"

"We're better off makin' as much noise as we can. Can't quite figure this critter out though. Cougars usually hunt at night or near dusk. And we've heard this one several times during the day. There's plenty of deer and other food for them so they shouldn't even look twice at us."

Maxine moved along at a fair clip and Annie had to hurry in order to keep up as they ducked under tree limbs and skirted fallen logs. She was tempted to ask Maxine to slow down, but then thought better of it since she couldn't quell the sense of urgency she was feeling about Louella Haven. Whether it was concern for the woman herself or something else, she couldn't say. Plus the afternoon session would be starting before long. "Do you think we should call out Louella's name?"

"I suppose it wouldn't hurt. Sounds carry out here." And so they both called Louella several times, with no response. Not from Louella; not from the cougar.

As they moved through the trees, Annie found herself wondering if perhaps the big cat was watching them. Several times she caught herself holding her breath and listening, but there was nothing. Not even the sighing of a gentle breeze or the buzz of a bee. It was an uneasy stillness that surrounded them. "Maxine, wait up."

The housekeeper stopped and half turned, waiting for Annie. "Sorry, didn't mean to leave you behind."

"Maxine, listen."

"I don't hear a thing."

"That's exactly what I wanted you to hear. Nothing. No birds, no bees, no breeze in the trees. Nothing. It's uncanny!"

They both stood there listening and hearing nothing.

Slowly Maxine began to nod her head. "Well, now. This spot does look sort of familiar, although I thought it was a lot farther back in the mountains."

Annie glanced around apprehensively. "You don't mean . . ."

Maxine sat down on a fallen log and wiped the sleeve of her shirt across her forehead. The area was absolutely still. Not even a grasshopper made its presence known. The only sign of life was the fading track of a passing jet plane high overhead.

Annie sank down beside Maxine onto the log. "For some reason, I'm absolutely weary."

"Arms and legs feel like they weigh a ton?"

"Exactly."

"Know what you mean. Might as well sit and rest a minute, because nothin's gonna bother us in here. In case you haven't noticed, we've got company." And Maxine nodded her head in the direction of Annie's left shoulder.

Lazing on a large rock maybe twenty yards away was a big cat. It watched them with serious concentration, tail twitching. Annie, when she could finally speak, found her voice came out a hoarse croak. "You said animals avoided this place."

"I said my old hound dog did and that there weren't any other tracks within the circle. Animals are supposed to avoid such places accordin' to legend. It's up to you whether or not you want to believe it. But notice he hasn't come any closer. He's stayin' outside the circle."

There was something almost chilling about the words *outside the circle.*

Brendan had had better luck at the Forest Service office than he had expected. They had many old maps and they let him look through them. At some time someone had arranged them according to year, and he had little trouble finding one that dated from about the time of Bertha Wing's wilderness trek. He'd discovered there were a good many caves and lava tubes in the region behind the resort. Brendan confined himself to that since it didn't seem likely Trilby's manager would have had the opportunity to venture too far away. He'd made a photocopy of the map and was now on his way to the library.

Someone else was on duty and she gave him the reference copy of Bertha Wing's journal. It didn't take him long to locate the section he wanted. While Wing gave a lengthy description of the area where she claimed to have seen the rock sculpture, it was of flora and fauna, not specific geologic features that might help him find it. Until he came to the very end of the chapter.

I noticed something unusual about the area not too far from the rock carving. In fact it was almost as if the stone maiden guarded this spot, although the fact she was on her knees made her posture seem more an act of supplication or sorrow. My horse, my companion for untold miles, refused to go any farther. It was then I noticed that it had grown unnaturally quiet. There was no birdsong, no insect sounds, nothing. Not even very much grew within the area my horse refused to enter. I am a woman who believes animals are to be heeded and so I turned her away from the spot. Later that afternoon when I set up my evening camp and went to write in my journal, I wondered about the unnatural place I'd found and resolved to learn more about it if I could. It seemed perfectly logical to me to assume that the woman bowed before the strange energy of the area my horse refused to enter. I never doubted that the presence of the one had resulted in the presence of the other. Will I ever know if she knelt in reverence or fear?

Brendan leafed through the remainder of the volume and found only one more reference to the sculpture and the area it guarded. Wing had made connection with an elderly Paiute woman who told her the area was haunted by spirits and that was why nothing ventured inside the circle. The rock maiden knelt in honor of these spirits.

Brendan knew he and Annie were now faced with two anomalies. To find one was to find the other, but finding either one was the problem.

Chapter Thirteen

Heart thumping, adrenaline pumping, mouth dry, Annie glanced around at the place where they found themselves trapped by the watchful cat. It was as Maxine suggested, almost a perfect circle. Nothing grew there—trees formed a half moon around it, but avoided, for some reason, the place where she and Maxine sat on a long-dead snag. Why? Was there something magical about the place where they found themselves, or was there something terribly wrong with it? The cat lazed on a large boulder, a rocky cliff with evidence of an old landslide off to one side.

"Maxine, we can't stay here forever."

"You've got that right. What would you suggest we do?"

"I was in hopes you might have a suggestion."

"Well, we could stay here until the cougar gets tired and goes home. Or we could trust dumb luck and just walk away. Maybe he's already had his lunch."

Annie glanced at her watch. "Oh, my gosh. It's past time for the afternoon session to start. And we still haven't found any sign of Louella." She was comforted to see her watch still worked. Then she realized the second hand wasn't moving. It had been past time for the workshop before they entered the circle.

"Did you ever think we might not want to find any sign

141

of her? Besides, little old Louella's whereabouts is the very least of my worries."

"Come on, Maxine. You don't seriously think . . ."

The housekeeper didn't let her finish. "That the cat might have gotten to Louella first? I don't know. Cougars are makin' a come-back, there are more and more sightings of them. A couple of women in California have been killed by cougars in recent years. But, on the other hand, food's plentiful in these mountains. So maybe he's just curious."

Maxine sounded calm enough, but Annie wondered if it was all facade. She didn't imagine the hard-working housekeeper ever admitted defeat easily. "Shall we test that theory by slowly backing away?"

"You want to step outside the circle?" Maxine made it sound as if they were defying some ancient ritual.

"You suggested that or outwaiting him. Frankly, he doesn't look like he has any place else he wants to be."

"Okay, let's move nice and easy," Maxine cautioned.

"Maxine, have you ever had any experience with cougars?"

"Let's put it this way, there's a first time for everything."

Annie tried to calm her breathing, to absorb the tranquility of the mountains surrounding them, to not reek of the fear that had settled like lead in the pit of her stomach. And to quell the idiotic urge to say, "Nice kitty, nice kitty," as they backed slowly away. Rightly or wrongly, Annie never took her eyes off the huge cat lolling on the rock near them, for all the world like an oversized housecat. So mesmerizing was the animal that she couldn't have looked away if her life had depended on it. What a scene this would make in a book if she and Maxine survived. If . . . If was a place she refused to go. Of course they would be all right. The cougar was sleek and looked well-fed. No doubt he was—as Maxine had suggested—simply curious.

As they backed out of the circle, the cougar rested its head on its huge paws and seemed to close its eyes. Annie wasn't at all convinced that the creature didn't watch them through narrow slits, well aware it commanded the situation and only slightly interested in what they were going to do. Maxine took hold of her hand. When Annie felt her trembling fingers she knew the housekeeper was as terrified as she was. Somewhere she had read that wild animals could smell your fear. If that were truly the case, then the aroma coming from them must be overpowering.

Once free of the barren circle, the trees closed around them and the last glimpse they had of the huge cat was that he snoozed—unconcerned about the vagaries of humans—in the sun. When they were well away from the circular clearing the two women exchanged glances. Maxine was the first to speak. "Okay—what do you say we make a run for it? Cougars are supposed to be put off by loud noises so it won't matter if we crash through the brush."

"Sounds like a plan to me." It seemed to Annie that they made enough noise to frighten anything away, but she didn't slow down to find out. Eventually she reached a point where she couldn't run any farther, had to stop or be sick. Maxine must have been feeling the same way because she didn't protest when Annie stopped, leaned her back against a Ponderosa pine, rested her hands on her knees, and gasped for breath. Only when her stomach settled in place and her breathing returned to normal did Annie look around at where they were. One tree might look like another, but Annie was pretty certain she'd never been in this spot before.

"Maxine, do you know where we are?"

"I was hopin' maybe you did."

The trees weren't as thick, the ground was rocky and uneven, and there was a lot more sky overhead. "We seem to be on higher ground. I thought I was out of breath simply because we'd been running, but I think we were also climbing."

"I think you might be right."

Suddenly it didn't seem so unlikely that years ago two women had walked away from the resort to take a hike and had never been seen again. From their current vantage point, it was obvious just how much wilderness area stretched beyond Whispering Pines Resort. There were rugged mountains, still with traces of snow even this late in the year, and vast tree-covered slopes as far as they could see. No visible roads were cut into the hillsides and certainly no buildings. In haste they'd gone looking for Louella Haven and in haste they'd retreated from the mountain lion. "Maxine, you don't think we're lost, do you?"

"I sure hope not because I'm thirsty as all get out." Maxine studied their surroundings. "I've hunted in this back country more times than I want to count, but it's like everything got turned around back there in that clearing. And then we did hightail it outta there in pretty haphazard fashion. I'm sure if we just stop and think about it, we'll get our bearings."

Annie lowered herself to a squat with her back resting against the tree. "So neither one of us has any idea where we are."

Maxine sat cross-legged on the ground, one knee poking through a hole in her jeans. "That could be the situation."

"Were we careless or stupid?"

"If they don't find us till spring you know what the newspapers are gonna say."

"Come on, Maxine. Let's see if we can figure a way out of this mess. We can't have come that far."

"Which doesn't mean we aren't lost. It's hot and I'm thirsty. So what do you say we walk downhill and get out of this sun."

"While we walk keep your eyes open for some sign we might have left. Broken limbs, branches, scuffed earth . . ."

Maxine grinned. "You sound like a regular Daniel Boone."

"Don't I wish." Annie kept her eyes open for any indication they were retracing their steps, but it was almost as if they'd been transported by air from one spot to another. A pair of hawks circled overhead, but otherwise there was no sign of life. She shaded her eyes with her hand and watched the gliding birds and then frowned as one of them seemed to be suddenly pushed away from its flight path. At the same time she heard an unusual sound she couldn't identify. She turned abruptly to Maxine. "Did you hear that?"

"Yeah, what was it?"

"I don't know, but it seemed to come from over there." And she pointed in the direction of the birds. "Let's investigate."

"Why?"

"Because maybe it might be something that would help us."

"It sure doesn't sound like it." But Maxine decided to follow Annie rather than run the risk of getting separated.

Annie was puzzled at what she was hearing. It was almost a breathing sound, and she stopped when she came to what she thought was the source. A large opening, almost like an air hole or skylight, was expelling cold air from inside the earth. The opening was somewhat restricted, although large enough that either of them could fall in, and ringed with red, pitted lava rocks interspersed with gritty dirt. This entrance descended straight into darkness, so it was impossible to tell how deep it might be. "Where do you suppose this leads?"

"Nowhere I want to go. But I've heard of this kind of cave. It's what they call a breather. On cold days it inhales and on warm days it exhales. Again it's one of those places old-timers talked about, but I never thought to see it. I must say, Annie, hangin' out with you is provin' to be very interesting." The rush of cool air pushed their hair away from their faces. Maxine edged forward and a small piece of ground gave way beneath her.

"Careful!" Annie automatically reached toward Maxine as if the gesture alone could halt any fall. But she would have been better off heeding her own warning when she lost her balance and suddenly pitched forward.

Chapter Fourteen

Brendan pulled up to the back door of the lodge, eager to share what he'd learned with Annie, but surprised to find not only Trilby but the other guests gathered there. Trilby rushed over to greet him as he stepped from the car. "Oh, Brendan—something awful has happened!"

It took Brendan only seconds to realize that Annie was absent from the throng. Trilby's exclamation that something awful had happened cut through him like a knife. "What do you mean something awful has happened? Where's Annie?"

"I don't know! She's missing and so is Maxine."

A tall, silver-haired woman with presence stepped forward. Brendan remembered she'd been introduced to him as Iris Barton. "Annie was concerned this morning because Louella never showed up for the morning session. I suspect she went looking for her. But that was over three hours ago."

Louella was very much in evidence and Brendan turned to her. She spoke before he had a chance to say anything. "I know! I know! I should have let Annie know I might not make it to the morning session."

Brendan didn't feel the need to be diplomatic. "Where were you?"

Louella looked away. "I went for a hike."

"You didn't feel inclined to get your money's worth?"

"I thought I'd be back in time." Louella definitely sounded defensive.

"So it pretty much is a given that Maxine and Annie went into the woods looking for Louella."

Everyone more or less nodded their assent, but Iris was the one who spoke up. "We became concerned about half an hour into what should have been the second session. Annie did not strike any of us as the kind of person who would simply neglect her responsibilities. Again Louella wasn't there, although she did show up eventually. She hadn't seen Annie so we went looking for someone—any-one—and the only person we could find was Trilby. Maxine was nowhere in evidence. Jackie recalled seeing the two of them talking together behind the resort and then she saw them walk into the woods. We assumed they went looking for Louella."

Brendan turned to Jackie. "Did you overhear anything by some chance?"

Jackie looked away and then down at her feet. "The window was open and they were making no effort to be quiet. It was obvious that Annie was worried about Louella but didn't want to go off into the woods by herself. She asked Maxine to accompany her. I could tell they didn't plan on being gone long."

"But you at least know the direction they were headed?"

"Yes." And Jackie pointed into the trees.

"Then I'm going to go looking for them."

Fran Shipman piped up. "What about our afternoon session?"

Iris gave her a withering look. "Obviously it's postponed for the moment."

Trilby stepped into the fray. "I'm sure Annie will make it up to everyone."

Brendan looked around at all of them, too worried about Annie to be even the least bit diplomatic. "Let this be an

example to all of you. This is a wilderness area. You're
here as a group. Because of the small number of you any
absence is noticed. It's common courtesy to let someone
know where you're going. Louella, it's been obvious to
several of us that you go somewhere at night. And then
yesterday and today you don't show up for the morning
session. Annie is concerned about each and every one of
you. It was thoughtless of you to think you could register
for the workshop and then go your own way without a word
to anyone. For the rest of you, I know Annie and I know
she'll make good on the workshop—refund your money if
you can't stay over an extra day. Extend the workshop for
those of you who can. Now, I'm going looking for the two
women and if I'm not back by dusk I want you to call the
police."

Iris stepped forward. "Maybe we shouldn't wait that
long. It's difficult to organize a rescue in the dark."

Brendan glanced at his watch and saw that it was three
o'clock. "I know, but I'm getting a late enough start as it
is. I need to try and find them."

"Would you like some company? I'm an experienced
hiker and two sets of eyes are better than one. Besides, I
have my cell phone with me. We could keep in touch with
the lodge—let them know what's going on."

"If we can get through, sure."

Jackie, shy by nature, always hesitated to suggest anything but piped up with, "Maybe you should leave a trail
of breadcrumbs so you don't get lost."

Fran, trying to make up for what she knew was her earlier callousness, agreed. "Maybe you should mark the
way."

"I'll run inside and get some rags." Trilby was in and
out within seconds and thrust a bundle of rags at Brendan,
who looked at them in disbelief.

Iris, her mouth twitching, took them. "I'll be in charge
of marking our trail. Let's be off."

Trilby laid her hand on Brendan's arm. "Be careful,

please. Too many people have disappeared into that back country." Her eyes were wide with fear and her chin trembled. Trilby was not at all the kind of woman Brendan admired, but she was Annie's friend and he thought she was genuinely concerned for their safety.

Brendan and Iris stepped into the woods and seconds later heard the chilling scream of a cougar. It momentarily stopped their breathing, but it was Brendan's stomach that knotted with apprehension. If anything happened to Annie he didn't know what he would do. It didn't matter if she signed his paychecks or even if she owned the world and he owned nothing. He loved her.

When it came time to tell her story, Annie would swear that her heart both stopped and then speeded up simultaneously. She reached out with flailing arms and grasping fingers in an effort to stop her fall into the dark pit of the breather. But there was nothing as she pitched forward. Nothing but the taste of fear and the certainty she was falling to her death. Cold air rushed past her as she fell, expecting each moment to smash against a rocky ledge or the bone-shattering floor of the cave. She heard someone scream, but couldn't say if it came from herself or from Maxine. Just that it seemed to trail her into the unknown that held her in its grip. To say that she was afraid was an understatement. She'd never been so afraid in her life. And then it was over.

Annie lay there unable to move, the wind knocked out of her, her heart hammering so hard she thought it might shatter, and rockets going off in her head. High above, the narrow opening of the cave seemed to spin and she closed her eyes against a rising tide of nausea. Was it minutes or simply moments before she realized she lay on something soft that didn't move or growl? She'd heard something snap when she hit bottom and had thought it was her. But a flexing of her limbs proved none of them were broken, and while it made her nauseated to move around, she could. So what had she broken in her fall? And in turn, what had broken her fall? She lay back down in the hopes that the sickness would pass. She kept her vision on the opening to the cave and saw a head appear.

"Annie, Annie, are you okay?" Maxine's voice, generally calm and matter-of-fact, bordered on panicky as it echoed within the cave.

Again Maxine called out. "Are you okay?"

Annie managed an affirmative mumble there was no hope Maxine could hear.

"Look, Annie, I'll get help. Don't move, don't go anywhere. I'll be back with help. Don't despair! Okay?"

Annie nodded much to her own regret when the rockets went off again in her head. Maxine couldn't see or hear her. Soon the housekeeper's head disappeared from view and Annie felt more alone than she ever had in her entire life. How was Maxine going to rescue her when they were already lost?

Annie kept hoping that Maxine would reappear, but when she didn't Annie thought she'd better see if there was anything she could do to help herself. There was some light coming from the skylight opening. When her eyes adjusted she was able to barely make out her surroundings and to discover what she had landed on. It was the remains of a very large bear. The thick hide had saved her from serious injury, and the breaking bone sound she'd heard must have been one of the skeleton's smaller bones. It was a relief to find that she wasn't seriously hurt, although she had no doubt she would be covered with scrapes and bruises when she was rescued. Rescue, a thought she would cling to for dear life. Not even for a minute would Annie let herself think that Maxine might not find her way back to the resort. Had the bear also fallen through the opening, or had it entered some other way and either been trapped or simply died?

She raised herself up on her hands and knees and peered around her. There was enough light that she could make out her immediate surroundings, and what she saw was chilling. Two names were scratched into the wall—Jane Barton and Frances Waters, 1952. Annie sat back down. Was it simply a coincidence that one of the women taking her writing workshop was also named Barton? Surely Iris would have said something if there were a connection. Still, it was a curious coincidence. She'd bet these were the two women who had disappeared from Whispering Pines. The date was about right. She shivered and rubbed her hands along her arms. Was it really cold or was she suddenly frightened that she would find something far worse than a bear carcass?

If only she had a light! And then she remembered the fire she'd tried to start that morning and the matches she'd stuffed into her pants pocket afterward. She dug them out and lit one of them, temporarily blinded by the flame that was brilliant in the near darkness of the cave. But she was reassured when she saw no remains other than those of the bear. The match burned down, singeing her fingers, and she dropped it, watching it fizzle out on the dirt floor. Again she glanced upward. Was it possible that she could climb out? While her fall had seemed to last forever, the opening to the cave wasn't really that far above her. But a careful search revealed no hand holds, no rocky ledges waiting to be gripped.

The cave or lava tube was tall enough for her to stand up in although she still felt headachy and whoozy. She was careful to watch where she put each foot, aware she could still hurt herself. The tunnel that moved away from the lighted well of the cave was narrow if high enough to stand up in, and so she felt her way along until there was no longer any light coming from the entrance. That was when she stopped and realized the sour taste in her mouth was real. While nothing was obviously broken, she was not in one hundred percent condition. Common sense argued that she return to where she'd landed and wait to be rescued. But she couldn't stand the pressure of sitting and waiting and doing nothing. She knew that was how people got irrevocably lost, but she had to see where this tunnel led, if perhaps it would take her into the open air. Never mind the daunting evidence of the two names etched into the wall. Two women who had disappeared never to be seen again. That would not happen to her. She would be found or she would rescue herself. Against high odds she had survived the fall and she wasn't alone. Maxine was about as resourceful as they came, and she had every faith that Maxine would make her way back to the lodge and bring help.

Meanwhile she would light another match and walk as far as its light would last, telling herself each step would be the last and that she would turn around. But each foot of ground covered encouraged her onward until finally she was down to her last two matches and had no idea how far she'd come. So far there had been no further evidence of the women who'd left their names on the cave wall. Perhaps she had mistakenly assumed they were the women who had disappeared from the resort. No doubt many people had explored this cave over the years, although she would assume they'd found an easier access. This kept her moving forward to the other entrance she hoped to find.

The last match burned out and she blinked, wondering if she was seeing an afterimage of the flame, then realized with a thumping heart that she was literally seeing a light at the end of the tunnel. Her first inclination was to rush forward, but she was able to rein in that impulse while continuing ahead one cautious step at a time. The floor of the lava tube was rough and uneven and she didn't need to fall when she might be so close to escape. The opening might be too small for her to fit through and so there was no sense in getting overanxious. But she couldn't help herself. And those were very real tears of joy and gratitude when she reached the end of the tunnel and saw that she could possibly squeeze through.

The rocks scraped against her back and she had to grit her teeth against the pain, but she was going to make it, although she almost died of fright when someone took her hand. "Here, let me help you."

She was battered, bruised, but free when she stood up and faced the man who had taken her hand. Together they stood under a ledge overhang where she could see he had set up camp. "I recognize you!" It was the elderly man from the Log Cabin Café.

"And I recognize you. You're the woman with more curiosity than what's good for her. What are you doin' crawlin' around in there? How did you even get in there in the first place? I've been here all day."

"I fell."

"You fell?"

"Through a skylight entrance."

"So there's another way in, is there?"

"Certainly not one I'd recommend. It was quite a drop."

"You were lucky you didn't break your neck."

"I'm well aware of that, but I landed on an old bear carcass. His thick pelt saved me from serious harm. However—do you mind if I sit down?" Now that she was safe, she could admit, to herself at least, how frightened she'd been—and how lucky.

He quickly took a hold of her and supported her while she sank to the ground. "Would you like a cup of coffee?"

"Please. . . ." Annie hoped she wasn't going to disgrace herself by being sick now that she was rescued. The man handed her a tin cup brimful of coffee into which he'd poured a generous dollop of canned milk and a spoonful of sugar. It tasted better than she could ever have predicted. "*Who* are you? I mean, what's your name?"

"Who do you think I am?"

"I have no idea, unless you're the person Trilby thinks is threatening her and breaking into the lodge."

"A man can't be accused of breaking into a place that's rightfully his." He took a gulp from his own cup and watched for her reaction. "She's trespassin' on my property and I want her out."

"It can't be your property."

"And why not?"

Impossible as it seemed, there was only one person who might logically have a claim to Whispering Pines. But why would he skulk about in the woods? "How old are you?"

"Old enough to be who you think I am."

She wanted to say, *Not so fast*, but settled for, "You're claiming to be the missing son, Wilbur Watkins."

"Guilty as charged."

"Why have you come back after all this time? Why not sooner?"

"Because I didn't remember who I was or where I was from until not too long ago. I'd carried these keys around with me all these years, knowin' they had to fit somewhere, and when I finally remembered I came home."

"Keys to the lodge?"

"That's right."

Annie leaned forward, extending her cup for a refill although she shook her head at more canned milk. "But why didn't you walk up and introduce yourself to Trilby? She is, after all, related to you by marriage."

"She's trespassin' on my property and I want her outta there." He was stubborn if nothing else.

"But Trilby is—was—married to your brother's grandson."

"I don't care who she was married to. That lodge is mine and I intend to finish out my days there."

"Surely the two of you could work out something that would suit you both."

"What would suit me is for her to leave. I can't afford no lawyer, but I want her gone. If I wanted to live with her I wouldn't be holed up here in the woods."

"And what will you do with the lodge?"

"Live there—just as I did when I was growin' up. It's my home, not that woman's."

If his claim was valid, would Trilby lose everything she'd poured into the resort?

Annie had no sympathy for someone who made threats, anonymous or otherwise. "Mr. Watkins, Trilby may very well have a stronger claim to the resort than you. Especially if your mother left it to your brother. She did think you were dead."

He was definite on that point. "Nope, she woulda left it to both of us. No matter what. I was her favorite and she never woulda done me out of my inheritance. But I can see you and I are never goin' to see eye to eye on this matter so I might as well be helpin' you back to the lodge. And I'll ask you to keep my secret for now."

"You expect me to keep quiet when you have my friend on the verge of an emotional breakdown? No way will I keep your presence or your identity a secret." No sooner were the words bravely spoken than Annie wondered if they'd also been foolishly spoken. After all, she was alone with him in a section of forest he knew well and she didn't. And no one knew where she was. Quickly, she added, "I will however, arrange a meeting between you and Trilby. I'll even lay the groundwork so you can come to some kind of mutual agreement. If you agree to that, I'll keep your identity to myself until the guests leave. But you have to also promise not to leave Trilby any more warnings."

He wasn't about to budge. "I don't want to meet with her. I just want her outta my place."

"Mr. Watkins, you've done me a favor by helping me, but I think you're being unreasonable. You're harassing a perfectly nice woman who has had her own share of bad luck recently. You have her afraid, nervous, unable to concentrate because of your childish threats. You need to re-alize and accept that there is an alternative to what you've been doing."

"I lost fifty years of my life not knowin' who I was and livin' away from home. Well, I'm back now and I want my home back. And that's that." He walked her to the lake, paddled her across in his canoe, and helped her onto the shore. "Can you make it the rest of the way on your own?"

"I think so. Thanks. . . ."

"No thanks necessary—just keep quiet about me and why I'm here." With that, he stepped into his canoe and paddled back across the lake, leaving Annie to wonder if he really expected her not to say anything. And leaving her to wonder when would be the best time to break the news to Trilby. She didn't think the man claiming to be Wilbur Watkins posed any kind of physical threat. Therefore she decided since the workshop was winding down that she could safely wait until it was over to say anything. It didn't seem appropriate to drag those attending into the middle of Trilby's problems. And she could well imagine the emotional outburst that would follow the revelation of the old man's identity.

If Annie had been a returning hero, she couldn't have asked for a warmer welcome when she limped into the clearing behind the lodge. Everyone gathered around her wanting to know what had happened, but they were elbowed aside by Maxine who had just returned herself only moments before. The housekeeper—her partner in adventure—gave her a bear hug.

"How'd you get out of that cave? I like to broke my neck and a speed record gettin' back here for help. I guess pure instinct sent me in the right direction."

Trilby was next in line to give her a hug, but even as she did Annie wondered what the man in the woods's claim would ultimately mean for Trilby. "We've been worried sick. Brendan and Iris went looking for the two of you. What in the world happened?"

Annie saw that Louella was part of the crowd. "I was worried about Louella. So I thought I'd go looking for her during the break, but I didn't think I should go on my own since I'm not at all familiar with the woods around here. I asked Maxine to go with me. And no pun intended, but it's a wilderness out there and we somehow got turned around."

Jackie Marks chimed in, "But you're all cut and bruised and you're limping!"

Annie and Maxine exchanged looks. "Well, that is another story."

Carmen Potts rested her hands on her ample hips. "You can't refuse to tell us. Not when we've been so worried. It wouldn't be fair."

"Oh, we'll tell it. But I'd like to wait until everyone is here so I only have to tell it once."

Maxine gave a wave of her hand. "You do the tellin', Annie. That's your line, not mine. I'm gonna go home and fix dinner for my kids. A houseful of screamin' kids seems pretty tame after what we've been through. See y'all tomorrow."

It was definitely reunion time, because Brendan and Iris emerged from the trees, both of them wearing defeated looks until they caught sight of Annie. Brendan was at her side instantly and not at all embarrassed to hug her with everyone looking on. "Where have you been? I've been worried sick. My God, woman, you scared the life out of me. Whatever possessed you to go off without me?"

"You weren't here and I was concerned about Louella. Look, I'll be happy to tell all—once I've had a chance to clean up and get something to eat. I'm starved!"

Brendan took charge. "I think that's an excellent idea. Trilby and I'll get dinner on the table and you can explain everything then." He used a tone of voice that no one was apt to argue with.

Annie limped up to her room and was appalled when she saw herself in the mirror. It was a miracle that she had survived her fall without breaking anything. Her guardian angel deserved a vacation after today. She showered, treated her scrapes and bruises, put on clean clothes, and went back downstairs, ready to tell everyone an abridged version of her adventure. Later she would tell Brendan about meeting the old man and what he'd told her.

Annie insisted they eat first and then she'd tell her story. She didn't know when she'd seen a bunch of people gulp down their food so fast. She couldn't help but notice that

Louella had been uncharacteristically quiet and that the others, while they weren't rude to the older woman, also didn't go out of their way to engage her in conversation. The woman was there as part of a group and she'd owed them an explanation if she was going to be absent from the proceedings.

Finally it was Fran who asked, "Well, do we get to hear the story or not?"

Annie drew in a deep breath. "Ah, yes, the adventures of two silly women. Or a more compelling title might be the adventures of Maxine, Annie, and the cougar." There were the expected gasps and Brendan's mouth-tightening frown. "As you all know, I was worried about Louella and so I thought I'd see if I could find her over the break. I asked Maxine to accompany me since she'd told me she and her late husband used to hunt this area." Annie then proceeded to fill them in on events, excluding the man who claimed he was Wilbur Watkins. She noticed that Louella watched her intently. The possibility occurred to Annie that there might be some connection between the two.

"Could you find that area again, the one animals avoided?" Frank Potts wanted to know.

"I'll be honest with you. I don't know if I could or not. I should be able to explain what it was like, but I can't. Other than to say there was something confusing, almost turned around about the area. We couldn't seem to get our bearings. I'm not so sure I'd want to locate it again." And she gave an involuntary shiver.

"I did find evidence of the two women who disappeared from here all those years ago. At least I found two names scratched into the wall of the cave, and the date was right."

Jackie shivered. "Did you find any bones?"

"No, none."

"Do you think the exhaling air cushioned your fall somewhat?" Jocelyn asked.

"I hadn't thought about it, but I don't suppose it's impossible. Let me tell you, it was an experience."

"Do you think you could find this cave again?" Frank Potts definitely was interested in locating where Annie and Maxine had been.

"At this point, I don't even want to try." Annie didn't want to be put in the position of getting them all lost. And she wasn't at all sure she could find the cave or the circle again.

"Annie, are you certain there was something unusual about this place you found? Maybe the cougar left you alone because he'd already fed."

Annie glanced over at Brendan. Was he trying to be logical or did he want her to disclaim the strangeness of the area where she and Maxine had encountered the cougar?

"That's always possible, I suppose." Nevertheless she had experienced the unusual atmosphere of the spot and no amount of reasoning could change that reality. "We'll have to see. Now I really am tired. I do want you to know that I will make up the afternoon session either by extending your time here or by refunding part of your fee. I'll leave that choice up to you and we can discuss it in the morning." Annie pushed her chair back from the table. "Tomorrow's another day, I'll see you all then."

Annie headed for the kitchen and hoped Brendan would follow. Which he did. "Close the door behind you. I have something to tell you and I don't want anyone to overhear me."

"I figured there was more to the story than you'd told."

"Do you know me that well?"

Brendan said, "I've come to recognize the little hesitations that signal you're leaving something out."

Annie sat down at the round table. "Could I get you to heat me a cup of warm milk, please? That is if you don't mind. I think it'll help me sleep and weary as I am, I ache so that I'm not sure I'll be able to get to sleep without a little help." She rested her head in her hands and battled with an absurd urge to either laugh or cry. Both seemed to border the edges of her consciousness.

"I'd be glad to fix you some warm milk. I might even join you. You were living the adventure but I never want to be as worried about you again as I was today." He came around behind her to rest his hands on her shoulders and she leaned her head against his arm. "Don't ever do anything like that again, please. You could have broken your neck falling into that cave. You're not some cat with nine lives, you know."

She took his scolding in the spirit it was meant—as one person caring for another. "I didn't think at the time I was taking any chances. But yes, I don't intend to repeat today if I can help it."

"Then how about sharing with me what I know you didn't tell the others? Then I'll enlighten you with the results of my junket to town."

"Maybe you should go first."

Brendan shook his head. "No way! You talk, I'll heat the milk."

"Brendan—some of it is almost unbelievable." She glanced around. "I'm not even sure I should tell it to you within shouting distance of the lodge. If any walls have ears, it's bound to be these."

"You're not going to get off that easy."

"I'm not trying to evade the issue, I just don't want to be overheard, because the situation here might not be what I thought it was—what we thought it was."

"Has something changed?"

Annie nodded and took a sip from the cup of warm milk he placed in front of her. Then she started to tell Brendan the details of everything that had happened. Hearing a sound outside the door, she paused and put her finger to her lips and pointed.

Brendan stood up, walked over, and pulled open the door. Trilby stood there, leaning forward at an angle so it was obvious she was eavesdropping. Hastily she tried to explain, "I was just wondering who was in the kitchen and whether or not I should interrupt."

Annie finished off her hot beverage and stood up. "I wanted some warm milk to help me relax. I'm off to bed now."

"That makes two of us." Brendan said. Neither one of them gave Trilby the chance to ask questions.

He walked her to her room. "Do you want to wait until tomorrow to tell me the rest of the story? We could take an early morning walk."

"I'd like that. It would help walk off some of the stiffness I'm sure to feel. The warm milk is doing its job and I really have passed the point of exhaustion and wanting to talk."

He gently touched the bruise on her cheek and then lightly kissed her on the lips. "Whatever works for you, Annie, works for me."

She smiled at his comforting words. They were a welcome lifeline as she tried to coax sleep by working through the day's troubling revelation.

Chapter Fifteen

When Annie awoke the next morning it felt as if every bone in her body ached. Her sleep had been punctuated by a series of troubling dreams, and the unease they caused spilled over into wakefulness. Perhaps a hot shower would get her going, but oh, what she wouldn't give at the moment for a bathtub to soak in and a day free of commitments. Since neither one of those were attainable at the moment, she settled for the shower.

She'd just gotten dried off and dressed when she heard a knock on the door. Hoping it was Brendan, she went to answer it. "Good morning."

"How are you feeling this morning?"

"Sore, but I think a cup of hot coffee and a walk to the lake with my favorite guy might make me feel better."

"I think I can accommodate both requests. The coffee should be ready by the time you get downstairs." And he brushed tousled hair away from her face.

Annie combed her hair and applied just a touch of makeup. Her scrapes and bruises were still very much in evidence and probably would be the focal point of her appearance for several days to come. And she hurt—everywhere. She carefully closed the door to her room behind her and quietly made her way to the kitchen. She didn't want to meet up with anyone any sooner than necessary.

Brendan handed her a thermal mug full of coffee. "Let's be off before anyone else is up." They talked little as they hiked to the lake. The air carried a chill that suggested winter weather was getting impatient to put in an appearance. Once they'd arrived at their destination, they each picked out a comfortable stump to sit on. "Okay, Annie, tell me what you left out last night."

"Do you think Trilby was actually eavesdropping on our conversation?"

He nodded. "Probably."

"Brendan, the elderly man camping on the other side of the lake claims to be Wilbur Watkins!"

"No!" But even as he protested Brendan realized it wasn't impossible. "He actually told you that?"

"He did, and he claims the resort is his. He's behind the threatening notes and messages. I tried to reason with him, to convince him to meet with Trilby and work things out. But he insists the lodge is his and she's trespassing no matter who she might have married." She took a sip of warming coffee.

"Annie, I don't know about this. Where does he say he's been all these years?"

"He claims he was injured during World War II and had amnesia until recently. But that he'd carried a set of keys with him all these years because he felt they were a link with who he really was. Naturally they were a set of keys to the lodge. That's how he gets in and out. So Trilby hasn't been imagining that."

"Why in the world doesn't he just introduce himself? Why all the cloak-and-dagger melodrama? Unless he knows his claim wouldn't hold up under much scrutiny and he feels the only way to gain possession of the resort is to force Trilby out."

"You think he might be lying then?"

"I think he bears investigating before we say anything to

Trilby. We need more than his word that he's who he says he is."

Annie glanced at her watch—it was now in perfect working order—and got reluctantly to her feet. She was still feeling the aftershock of yesterday's adventure. "I need to be getting back. The workshop wind-up session starts in forty-five minutes and I owe it to everyone to be on time. Or they'll think I'm as bad as Louella. Walk back with me and tell me what you learned yesterday in town."

As they walked along, occasionally encountering a shower of golden aspen leaves, Brendan told Annie what he'd uncovered. "There are many caves and lava tubes in this back country. I was able to get a photocopy of a map, circa about the time Bertha Wing rode through, that should help us locate the cave we think we see in her sketch. I think it's the same one you fell into. And I'll explain why in a minute. I also took another look at Bertha Wing's journal. This time I found out what—given your adventure of yesterday—we need to know to find the rock carving of the Native American woman."

"Brendan, that's wonderful!"

"Wing mentions it was on the other side of a small clearing her horse refused to cross. When we compare Wing's drawing with the one done by Trilby's manager I think we'll find your cave is the one visible in Wing's drawing and replaced by a landslide in the manager's. According to an elderly Paiute woman that Wing interviewed, the rock carving has always been there, so we'll probably never know its origin. However, the rock carving rests outside a sacred circle that is avoided by all except the spirits."

"And careless hikers like Maxine and me. That sounds like the place. And there was a large rock. The cougar was lying across it so I never got a look at the other side."

"Think you might be able to find this spot again?"

"Think I'm sure gonna try. If at all possible, I'm not leaving here without a look at that carving. To think that Maxine and I were so close yesterday."

"I've traced a fairly simple route on the map that I think will take us in the right direction." He was silent a moment and then added, "While you're winding the workshop up today, I'm going back into town. There's some more research I want to do at the library."

"Oh, what?"

"Don't get your hopes up, but I'm going to try and track down whether or not our backwoods friend is telling the truth about who he is. Plus there's a hunch I want to follow up."

"Is it a very big library?"

"Adequate for the size of the town—and they'll have what I need. Along with the added advantage that I won't be interrupted by anybody from here. I don't want the wrong person getting suspicious until I know if my hunch is going to pay off."

"And you're not going to tell me any more than that?"

"Not until I know more for sure." He gave her a wide grin. "Sorry, but what I suspect is rather improbable. I don't want to get your hopes or your curiosity up unless there's good reason. But you'll be the first to know if I'm guessing right."

Everyone was present for the final session. It was supposed to last only half a day, but by mutual agreement they extended it. "We're going to spend a lot of time writing because I want you to go home with the complete outline for a mystery novel," Annie told them. "With that goal in mind, I want you to come up with three suspects, their relationship to the victim, and good reasons why each of them could have committed the murder. Follow that with substantial alibis for two of them. The remaining suspect is your killer."

Louella had surprised Annie by attending the last session and was now loading her car preparatory to leaving. Everyone else except Iris, who stood beside her on the front porch, had already gone.

"Louella seems to be almost on her way and so now I suppose it's time to ask you to show me that cave. I think you can understand why *I* need to visit it. I didn't really want to ask while anyone was around, because I didn't want anyone else tagging along."

"You want to go now? Today?"

"I can't stay over." There was a note of obstinacy in her voice. "You *must* know why it's so important to me. And knowing that, how can you refuse me?"

Indeed, how could she? "There were two names scratched on the wall of the cave. Jane Barton was one of them. What was her connection to you?"

"She was my mother."

Annie was plainly surprised and Iris chuckled, correctly interpreting her thoughts. "I'm older than I look. I was a precocious eight-year-old when my mother—disappeared. I can still remember her telling me that she was off on an adventure that was going to make us rich and famous. It was just the two of us by then; my father was long gone. She was going to expose the Whispering Pines Resort health spa—silence the rumors by finding out the truth. She promised to bring me a surprise. She never promised that she wouldn't come back at all. So, Annie, I will either go with you or without you, but I will go today. And what are my chances of success without you? What happened in that cave changed my life and I've some ghosts to finally put to rest. My mother's choices just didn't put her life at risk."

"What happened to you, Iris? After you lost your mother?"

"A stern-faced grandmother appeared and whisked me away. She firmly believed if you spared the rod, you spoiled the child. So—how soon can we be on our way?"

Annie knew Brendan had marked a route on the old map he'd photocopied. If he'd left it in his room then she just might be able to locate the place where Jane Barton had disappeared. Otherwise she wasn't sure she could find it. However, she was not unsympathetic to Iris's wishes. "We can leave in the length of time it takes us to get ready. But bear in mind I can't guarantee success."

Brendan was surprised to see both Louella's and Iris's cars still parked in front of the lodge when he returned. He'd thought everyone would have left by now. In fact, he'd been counting on it. He was eager for the opportunity to confront the man who claimed to be Wilbur Watkins and he wanted Annie with him. It was quiet inside the lodge and he wondered where everybody was. With five women in the building, you'd have thought there'd be some signs of activity.

The kitchen seemed to be a gathering place and so he headed in that direction, but Trilby was the only one there.

"Oh, Brendan—hi."

"Where's everyone?"

"Annie and Iris went to find the cave."

"You're kidding."

"No, Iris was adamant about seeing it before she headed home. It turns out her mother was one of the two women who disappeared all those years ago."

"And they just had to go today?"

"I guess Iris couldn't stay over."

"Did Louella go with them?"

"No, she left when everyone else did."

"Then why is her car still parked out front?"

"Are you sure?"

"Positive. There's no mistaking that old Dodge."

Trilby dried her hands on a dish towel. "Then she must have come back for some reason. I'll see if I can find her."

"Find who?" Neither of them heard Maxine come into the room.

"Maxine, have you seen Louella?"

"I saw her out back just a little while ago. I was surprised to see her 'cause I thought she'd left. I figured maybe she'd forgotten something, but then she headed off into the timber."

"That's odd."

Brendan took Trilby's comment a step farther. "It's more than odd. Look, I'm going to follow Annie and Iris. If Louella turns up, which I don't think she will, try to keep her here until I get back."

"Annie said I was to tell you if you returned before they did, and that she'd taken your map. I guess that makes sense to you."

"Yes, that's good news. At least that way they shouldn't get lost." He'd worked so long on the map that he could easily walk from memory the route he'd plotted. And there was little doubt in his mind that Louella was somewhere close behind Annie and Iris.

Chapter Sixteen

Annie and Iris hiked single file, saying little, simply enjoying the possibility of discovery. Annie carried the map in her hand, being careful to follow the bends and curves Brendan had traced across its surface. And also being careful to recognize landmarks from the day before. Brendan had located the lake beyond the lodge, and using it as a reference point sited the resort and then traced a route from there.

"This landscape reminds me of the Cederberg Mountains in South Africa. I hiked there with a group I'd also been with on safari. They were great except for one obnoxious woman. I think we all would have gladly pushed her off the trail. As it turned out she tripped, fell, and was seriously injured." Iris's tone was quite matter-of-fact.

Annie wasn't sure how to respond. "That's too bad."

"Not really. We were well rid of her and could enjoy the rest of our trip without her constant complaining."

The trail they hiked took them gently upward, followed a rushing stream, and past a foaming waterfall. A much less circuitous and far lovelier route than she and Maxine had taken.

"What's that sound?"

Annie stopped on the trail, shifted her day pack to a more

169

comfortable position, and listened. "That's it! That's the cave. Maxine explained to me that it's known as a breather. On cold winter days it inhales and in hot weather it exhales."

"And that's where my mother died?"

"That's where I saw her name scratched into the wall."

"But you found—nothing?"

"That's right, but you must remember I had no light except a book of matches. So my range of vision was definitely limited."

Within a short length of time they reached the skylight drop into the cavern. Iris approached it cautiously. "I want to go down there. You can understand that, can't you?"

"Iris . . . it's dangerous. And what would putting yourself at risk accomplish?"

"It would put my mind at rest. Prove to myself once and for all that my mother hadn't abandoned me on purpose."

"Did you ever really think that?"

"Often. I had to have been an encumbrance to a free spirit like my mother. There were many times when I wondered if she didn't simply walk into a new life."

"I don't think you have to worry about that. I think she and Frances Waters were trapped during an earthquake. The cave entrance was unstable and collapsed. Maybe their remains are somewhere in the cave or maybe under the landslide. We might never know exactly where they are."

"That's where you're wrong, Annie. I know exactly where Jane is buried."

Startled, they turned in unison to discover Louella.

Annie was the first to speak. "I thought you'd left."

"I was all set to leave, but then I overheard you agree to take Iris to the cave. It was an opportunity I couldn't miss. The reason I came to Whispering Pines. You wondered where I disappeared to everyday. I was searching for this very spot. I was so sure I could find it without any trouble. I was wrong. Fifty years is a long time, landscapes change, memories blur. I needed to bring my life full circle, and until I overheard you two talking I thought I was going home in defeat."

"But why? Why is the cave so important to you?"

Louella ignored Annie's question and spoke instead to Iris. "Iris, your mother loved you dearly. You were her favorite topic of conversation. She would never have abandoned you. I, on the other hand, had a dangerously possessive husband and a stagnant career. Mother Nature gave me the opportunity to start over again, and I seized it."

"You're Frances Waters?" Annie was incredulous.

"I am—yes."

Brendan reached them just as Louella confirmed his suspicions about her identity. At one point he'd thought she might be connected with the man calling himself Wilbur Watkins. But when he tried to come up with a reason for her back country rambles, he began to wonder if she could be one of the women who'd disappeared so long ago. A perusal of old newspapers at the library had provided not only a thorough knowledge of that disappearance, but also photographs of both women. Fifty years was a long time, but Louella still bore a resemblance to the young woman she'd been then. He said nothing, just stood there, slightly out of breath due to the pace he'd set himself, listening to Louella's confession.

"We were in the cave when the quake struck. I got out, but Jane didn't. She's buried under that rock slide."

Iris took a step toward her. "And you left me to grieve and wonder why my mother had left and where she might be?"

"She was dead—and I wanted people to think I was also. It never occurred to me that you might think your mother had abandoned you. I'm sorry. I don't know what more I can do or say."

Iris turned away and Annie saw her wipe a hand across her eyes. Iris then drew in a deep breath and walked over to stand on the rim of the skylight entrance. Her proximity to the edge alarmed Annie, who moved to intercept her.

Annie hadn't taken more than a couple of steps when Brendan stopped her by placing a hand on her arm. After a brief hesitation, Iris took something from her pocket and dropped it into the cave. Then she started back the way they'd come. Without a backward glance at either Brendan or Louella, Annie followed.

Iris had loaded her car prior to leaving on the hike. Upon returning to the lodge, she went immediately to it, pausing only to say thank you to Annie, before driving away.

Minutes later Louella extended her hand to Annie before getting into her own vehicle. "Thank you for giving me the opportunity to bury my ghosts. They've been whispering in the back of my mind for a long time." Then she turned to look in the direction Iris had driven. Only a plume of dust remained. "Do you think she'll ever forgive me or understand why I did what I did? I never meant to hurt her."

"I think in time she will. Iris is a strong woman."

"I hope you're right. Well, I guess this is good bye."

Annie watched as Louella drove away, unprepared for the overwhelming combination of wonder and relief that filled her. "Who would ever have guessed?"

"At the secrets people carry around inside of them?"

Annie looked up at Brendan. "Apparently this was a secret you suspected. Why didn't you tell me you'd connected Louella with the women who disappeared?"

"Because I hadn't really. It was just a hunch that turned up during the night. I couldn't sleep, worrying in retrospect about what could have happened to you. So I tried to divert my thoughts by coming up with reasons Louella would go hiking rather than attend a workshop she'd paid good money for. Especially as her car and clothes seemed to indicate she's none too prosperous. At first I thought she might be connected with Wilbur Watkins. Then I decided differently when I noticed the direction she always took. It was away from his camp. Unless she walked the route she did to throw us off her trail. So what else would take her into the back country—an elderly woman who seemed to have a purpose. Even if it wasn't the one she said she'd come for.

"That was when I decided she might be connected with the mystery that seemed to haunt everyone's imagination. Not the stone carving, but the two women who had disappeared. You know we'd joked about the possibility they'd walked into another life. Well, I began to take that possibility seriously. I did the math and realized Louella was the right age to be one of those two women. All that remained was to look up some old newspapers, familiarize myself with all aspects of the disappearance, and study some pictures of the two women. Fifty years may have come and gone, but the Louella of today is recognizable as Frances Waters."

"I'm impressed, Brendan. You're a far better detective than I ever thought of being."

"Not at all. I may have done the research, but you're the one who did the leg work. It was your misadventures that pointed me in the right direction."

"So the fate of the two missing women is now laid to rest. What about Wilbur Watkins? Did you learn anything about him?"

"It's amazing what you can find on the Internet. Particularly with a little time and ingenuity. I followed a lot of tracks, but I eventually turned up proof that Wilbur Watkins is dead. He passed away eight months ago."

"Eight months ago? Where has he been all this time? And how in the world did you know you had the right Wilbur Watkins? There have to be a lot of people with that same name."

"True, but I typed in his name and worked my way through the list that came up. Surprisingly, there weren't that many. When I came upon an obituary that had to be his I knew I'd hit the jackpot. There was no attempt at subterfuge. It listed his place of birth, his military service, and his parents' names."

"But why didn't he ever come home?"

"That I can't answer. But maybe Donald Climber can."

"Who in the world is Donald Climber?"

"I'm pretty sure he's our Wilbur Watkins wannabe."

"And how did you arrive at that conclusion?"

"The obituary I came across listed his last place of residence. It was a home for retired sailors. I bought a prepaid phone card and placed a phone call. The manager of the facility was more than willing to talk to me. It seems Wilbur and Climber shared a room. I imagine they exchanged a lot of information about their past lives. Wilbur died eight months ago and Climber left a month after that. No forwarding address, nothing. They put the few things he'd left behind in storage. When I described our man to them they seemed to think he was Climber."

"So now all we have to do is confront him."

"Tomorrow we'll do just that. I don't think we should say anything to Trilby until after we've talked to him. It seems I've discovered the truth, but until we know for sure we'd better entertain the possibility that I could be wrong."

The mornings were progressively cooler and the next day was no exception. Brendan and Annie bundled up and headed for the camp on the other side of the lake. As they'd grown more familiar with the area, the distances seemed to shrink.

Brendan hoped an early morning visit would catch their prey still in camp, but no such luck. A smoldering fire suggested Climber hadn't gone far, but where and for how long was open to speculation. A battered coffeepot was snugged down in the coals to keep it warm. Surely an indication he'd be back soon.

Annie voiced her disappointment. "Do you suppose we'll have to hang around for very long in order to confront him?"

"If necessary, yes. I don't like men, no matter how old they are, who victimize women. Wilbur or Donald or who-ever he is has a lot to answer for and I intend to see he does." Brendan wasn't only angry for Trilby's sake, but for Annie's. Trilby's fear had brought them to Whispering Pines, had placed Annie in harm's way, and the man claim-ing to be heir to the property was to blame. Brendan clenched his fists in anger while reminding himself that he had the advantage of being probably forty-five years younger. If there was a confrontation it would have to be verbal.

The stillness was unsettling and Annie wondered if they were being watched, the purpose of their visit assessed. "Perhaps we should come back later." Much as she wanted to know the truth, she didn't have a good feeling about the situation.

"And give the old coot a chance to move on? No way!"

"I don't think that's likely since I doubt he even suspects we're on to him."

A stick snapped a warning and they turned to see the man claiming to be Wilbur Watkins approaching. "You're too late for breakfast, although I can offer you a cuppa coffee." There wasn't even the slightest suggestion he might have overheard them.

"This isn't a social call." Brendan's tone was clipped.

"Now that's too bad 'cause it gets mighty lonely out here."

"So, is it loneliness or just plain willfulness that led you to torment Trilby?" Brendan's anger was barely in check.

He glanced over at Annie. "She's tresspassin' on my property."

"That excuse won't fly. If you were who you claimed, you'd have been upfront about it. Trilby's a reasonable woman and I'm sure you could have come to an agreement beneficial to both of you. Something that would have left neither of you out in the cold. But instead you skulked around, breaking into the lodge, and subtly terrorizing

Trilby. So I began to wonder if you were someone with no legitimate claim to the resort. And that led me to discover who you really are."

The older man didn't look up from pouring himself a cup of coffee, but Annie thought she saw him hesitate while fumbling with the pot.

"I don't claim to be anyone other than who I am. So don't you go sayin' otherwise."

Brendan made eye contact before the older man shifted his gaze away. "I'm not in the habit of saying things I can't prove."

"Then I think you better keep your mouth shut."

Brendan sat down on a log and Annie sat beside him. She wasn't sure what she'd expected, but it wasn't this obvious belligerence. Sitting as close to Brendan as she was made it easy to feel the tension in his body. The man she still thought of as Wilbur Watkins was physically big and fit enough to survive for months in the woods. That made him more of an adversary than he might otherwise be. She was trying to think of some way to defuse the situation when Brendan spoke up.

"Tell me, Wilbur, are you very good with a computer?"

If the other man found the question unlikely he didn't let on. "Never worked one of the things in my life—and never wanted to." He sounded proud of the fact.

"Really? Then you might be surprised what you can find out about people. Like the fact Wilbur Watkins, the son of Elmira Watkins, died eight months ago. But then you knew that. The obituary listed his last place of residence. I gave them a call and it seems you fit the description of Wilbur's best friend. Did you really think you could pull off this charade, Donald?"

Expectation hung like campfire smoke in the morning air and Annie held her breath. Still, the older man's next move was unexpected. With a quick movement worthy of some-one half his age, he was on his feet and moving away from them. But not before flinging the coffeepot in Brendan's face. The lid flew off. Had he loosened it without them realizing it when he poured himself a cup? Brendan took the brunt of it full in his face. It wasn't scalding, but hot enough to be startling and he fell backwards off the log, taking Annie with him. She was first to recover and turned to help Brendan.

He waved her away. "I'm okay—don't let him escape."

Wilbur's imposter was headed uphill, away from the camp, and his progress was hampered by dry ground that gave way beneath his heavy boots. Later Annie would wonder at her presence of mind. She picked up a large rock, took aim, and threw it, hitting the fleeing man between his shoulders. He stumbled, fell, and slipped backwards which gave Brendan time to tackle him. Their scuffle was brief as they wrestled, rolling downhill toward the smoldering campfire. Annie watched in horror as they came to rest with Brendan's back against the embers. She looked around for a weapon, saw the coffeepot, grabbed it, and brought it down on the back of Climber's head with as much force as she could muster. As quickly as it began, the fight was over. The only sound against those of the forest was heavy breathing.

Annie helped Brendan push the other man away from him and then move away from the fire pit. Only then did she realize she was trembling, whether from fear or adrenaline she couldn't tell. "Are you all right? Your back . . ." And she brushed at the scorch marks on the back of his jacket as he sat up.

Brendan shook his head. "A little warm, that's all." He suddenly grinned at her. "Remind me never to underestimate you in a tight spot. I'm not sure how I would have fared without your help." He struggled to his feet and loomed over his opponent who was sitting up, but without any further show of resistance. "The game's up—you might as well admit it."

The elderly man shook his head as if to clear it, then sagged back against a log. "Okay, you win, although it's two against one—and me an old guy. But you gotta admit I gave it a good shot. Almost had myself a place to spend my last days other than an old man's home. You can't tell me that dizzy blond wasn't about to turn tail and run."

Annie was furious. "Don't you have any feelings of remorse?"

"Why should I? She was nothin' to me."

Brendan had all he could do to keep from slugging the guy. "What ever made you think you could get away with it?"

"Because I knew Wilbur better'n anybody. How he thought, why he did the things he did."

"Then why did he let his family think he was dead? From what we've been told, believing that almost broke his mother's heart."

"Yeah, at the last he kinda regretted that. He talked a lot about home. There wasn't much for us to do except sit around, play cribbage, and talk. That's when I learned Wilbur's life story. He was pretty badly wounded during WWII. The plane he was in went down in the Sea of Denmark and he washed ashore more dead than alive. Some farmers took him in and nursed him back to health. It was a long process, and by the time he was able to make it back to his unit he'd been listed as missing in action. The war was over and guys were bein' shipped home. Somehow his folks were never notified that he was alive. And that suited Wilbur just fine."

"Did he ever tell you why?"

Climber nodded. "He said he was his mother's favorite and she expected him to come home and help run this place. He had the wanderlust and didn't want to. He figured she had probably adjusted to his death and so he made a new life for himself, joined the merchant marine. It was only the last few months of his life that he got to thinkin' about home and wonderin' if it was still standin'. He talked about makin' the trip out, but he didn't live long enough. So I decided to make the trip for him. Even brought his ashes with me. Buried them in that grave out back of the lodge. What else did I have to do? And he'd left me what little money he had. Not much, but enough for a bus ticket out here—and back. He'd kept the keys to this place and a letter his mother had written him. It was pretty well worn, but the address was readable."

"You really thought the resort would be empty? Yours for the taking?"

"Not in the beginnin'. To start with I just wanted to see the place I'd heard so much about. What else did I have to do? Only when I got here and saw what a hash that blond was makin' of tryin' to run it did I get the idea of tryin' to move me in and her out. I figured with her gone I could enforce squatter's rights. Especially as I learned from other people's conversations that it had been empty for years before she moved in. Didn't figure anybody would do much investigatin' if she moved out. She hasn't made too many friends around here. Surprisin' how much you can learn by keepin' quiet and warmin' a back booth at the Log Cabin Café."

Annie didn't believe either Wilbur Watkins or Donald Climber were very admirable men. The feelings of others didn't seem to rank very high in importance in their scheme of things. To think Elmira Watkins spent what remained of her life mourning her irresponsible son caused Annie to blink back unexpected tears. "Were you the one who put the flowers on that memorial grave behind the resort?"

"Yeah, I thought that was a nice touch. You should have seen the look on that blond's face when she found 'em. Scared her silly, but they were only meant to honor Wilbur on dates I knew were important to him."

Annie discovered that both her hands and teeth were clenched tight. She couldn't quite believe his callousness and lack of remorse. Trilby wasn't a person to him. Simply a dizzy blond in the way of what he thought he wanted and deserved.

Brendan kicked dirt on the remains of the fire in hopes

of quelling the strong desire to slug Climber. "It shouldn't take you long to pack up and get out of here. I want you gone by noon. Otherwise we'll set the cops on you. Understand?"

Annie took one look at Brendan's expression and decided she certainly wouldn't have argued with his ultimatum. Apparently Climber thought the same thing, although it was with a noticeable lack of remorse for the trouble he'd caused. "Nights are gettin' too cold anyway. It's time to move on."

When Brendan and Annie walked into the lodge they could hear the vacuum running in the background. Annie assumed Maxine was busy cleaning up after the departed guests. Several days remained until the next workshop, but so far there were no takers. It puzzled Annie, but she knew there was nothing she could do about it.

Trilby was in the kitchen when they found her. Annie felt good knowing they had brought an end to the harassment against her. The look of relief that spread across Trilby's features when they told her what they'd discovered was reward enough for their efforts.

"How can I thank you two?"

Annie smiled. "There's no thanks necessary. But maybe you'll tell us why you refused to report the threats to the police. Your refusal never made much sense to me."

Trilby blushed. "I guess I do owe you an explanation, but it's almost embarrassing. I did report them at first, but the same officer answered every call and he made it quite obvious he thought I was crying wolf and seeking a little attention. He made it clear that he was willing to provide that attention. Perhaps I should have been flattered, but I wasn't. Quite frankly he frightened me a little. I was afraid to report him and bring more trouble to my front door. Anyway, I learned he was the only law enforcement in the area, so who would I have reported him to? I decided to live with the threats as long as I could."

"Oh, Trilby!"

"I know, I know. In retrospect I can see how foolish I was. And I should have told you in the beginning. I have no excuse other than what I did seemed like the right thing to do at the time."

The kitchen door opened part way and Maxine poked her head around the corner. "Sorry to interrupt, but I thought you might like to see what I found while I was cleanin' one of the rooms."

Puzzled they all followed her. Maxine explained as she led the way upstairs, "I don't know how I missed this before, but I did."

"Missed what, Maxine?"

"Just wait. You'll see." She led them into a room at the end of the hall. The closet door was open and a chair stood in the opening. "I was dustin' off the shelf, makin' certain nothin' had been left behind and found a loose board. Go on, Annie, stand up on the chair and take a peek."

Annie did as bidden, lifting the loose board to reveal a nest. "Is this a pack rat's nest?"

"I'd say so."

"My gosh!" There sparkled a diamond stud earring and the necklace she'd found in the ground near the hot springs. There was also a folded up piece of paper which she very carefully pulled free of the nest. She stepped down off the chair, giving Brendan a chance to have a look, while she handed Trilby the note.

Trilby gave a relieved laugh. "It's a farewell note from Big Al. He didn't disappear without a trace after all, but got a job offer more suited to his interests."

Maxine leaned over to read the note. "Where?"

"Managing the Osborne Working Studio and Gallery in Manzanita."

Annie glanced at Brendan. "That's not too far from where we live. Does he say anything else?"

"He says to keep the paintings and anything else he left

behind. To sell them if I want and maybe that will make up for any inconvenience caused by his hasty departure."

Maxine unwrapped a stick of gum from her seemingly endless supply. "Well, another mystery solved."

Epilogue

Annie sat on the front steps of Harbor House, stroking Tiga her cat, and enjoying what lingered of fall. The coast wasn't as colorful as the High Cascades, but the vine maple had outdone itself. She was glad to be home. She and Brendan had remained with Trilby the original length of time agreed upon, even though there were no more registrations for the workshops. They relaxed, hiked, and helped Trilby draw up a business plan. They'd enjoyed their time away, but Annie was glad to be home.

Brendan cut across the yard and headed in her direction. "Being lazy, enjoying the day, or both?"

"Both—but I have something I want to discuss with you."

He sat down beside her. "What?"

"I've begun to wonder—since we only filled one of the workshops we had scheduled for Whispering Pines—if perhaps I've saturated the market with mystery writing workshops."

"I doubt it. You always fill the ones here."

"No, no, hear me out." And she patted his knee. "I think we need to offer a variety of things—classes on non-fiction writing, biographies, have guest presenters, maybe even classes on cooking coastal cuisine."

"It's a possibility."

"I'd need a partner to make all this come together."

Brendan suddenly knew where she was going with this. "Maybe."

"No maybe about it. Definitely! I was thinking maybe you'd like to be that partner."

He looked directly into her eyes. "Only if that partnership contains words like 'I do and until death us do part.' Or however that goes."

"You know, I thought you'd never get around to asking."

"Well, I've asked, so what's your answer?"

"My answer is the same it would have been five minutes after we met. And that's yes."